MERRY LITTLE THINGS

LINDA SHANTZ

For Allison and her Labradors

ALSO BY LINDA SHANTZ

The Good Things Come Series:

Bright, Broken Things (a prequel)

Good Things Come (Book 1)

All The Little Things (Book 2)

All Good Things (Book 3)

This Good Thing (Book 4)

Merry Little Things (Book 5)

All The Best Things (Book 6)

Good Things Come Series: Books 1-3 Box Set

Good Things Come Collection: Books 1-5 Box set

For updates and bonus chapters, sign up for Linda's newsletter at
https://www.lindashantz.com/writes

CHAPTER 1

There was just enough snow covering the track's frozen surface to make the footing perfect, the steady vibration of the filly's exhaled breaths in concert with her muffled hoofbeats. *So silently, so silently.* They travelled in darkness, only the towering sulfur lamp on a hydro pole offering illumination.

The farm's training oval wasn't maintained this time of year. Why would it be? The racehorses were either getting time off now that the season in Ontario was almost over, or were in Florida for the winter. Not Reba though. Reba was Emilie's project.

No one else expected Reba to be a racehorse. She was too small. Too mild-mannered. Emilie believed, though. And if it turned out she was wrong, well, the little Thoroughbred was going to make someone a stellar riding horse — if Emilie could let her go.

She eased the compact chestnut and finished their session with a jog, turning in to face the white-blanketed infield. The filly's happy snort reverberated in the stillness as Emilie scrubbed her neck with a gloved hand. An eerie, solitary coyote howl, seemingly in answer, came from the dormant hayfields beyond the barns and pastures. Reba's head shot up, ears pricked, and she and Emilie gazed in the call's direction. *Just us loners out here in the wee hours.*

She hummed "All I Want For Christmas Is You" as they returned to the training barn, but didn't know if *you* was a guy or a friend; had two legs or four. All she knew was, this Christmas would be different. Because everything was different.

Stomping her feet in the barn aisle to knock loose the snow her boots had attracted, Emilie led Reba to her stall, still humming. The tune was stuck with her now. Earworm of the day. She left Reba nibbling hay while she returned the exercise saddle and bridle to the tack room.

"Coffee's on, Em."

Even though she'd figured the farm manager was around, his voice still startled her. Emilie set the saddle on a rack and hung the bridle on a hook. She'd clean both after she'd groomed Reba.

Austin Powers appeared in the doorway. Okay, Powers wasn't his real last name, but her soon-to-be brother-in-law had started calling him that and now Emilie couldn't un-think it. Austin had neither the movie character's smarmy charm nor the goofy look, and Emilie would never call him that to his face. Said almost-brother-in-law, Nate, had no such reservations.

"Thanks, but I'm helping Faye at the café this morning. I'll hold out for some real coffee."

Austin's hand went to the left side of his chest. "I'm hurt."

Emilie controlled her expression, and resisted the temptation to tell him *your heart isn't way over there, buddy.* "If you clean my tack, I'll bring you back a butter tart." She tipped off her helmet and stuffed the insulated beanie she'd worn under it inside it before hanging it up. The ball cap that replaced it, hiding her messy hair, was her favourite. It was navy and white with just a bit of orange, decorated with the New Chapter Thoroughbred Retirement logo. She repped the local aftercare organization every chance she got.

"Deal." There was no hesitation, Austin's grin immediate.

Emilie smiled in spite of herself. He wasn't unattractive. Five-ten or so. A light but sturdy frame. A pleasant enough face, though she wasn't a fan of the scruffy beard. His brown eyes caught the light of the overhead bulb and a Toronto Maple Leafs toque covered his curly dark hair. But... no. Even if she ignored his hockey allegiance. It hadn't been wise to say anything that might be misconstrued. Give the guy a crumb... She scooped up the grooming kit and escaped to Reba's stall.

She always felt she had to be careful about everything she said to him. Not like Nate, with whom she could freely flirt without fear of misinterpretation. Because Nate was marrying her sister. The ongoing tête-à-tête Emilie had with him far predated that impending event, but Nate had always been into Liv — as much as he might try to deny it. Emilie didn't have an older brother, or a brother at all, so she cherished the way he treated her like a younger sibling. The problem was, she ended up feeling like a little sister to all the guys in her sphere, including the ones she dated. At least Austin didn't treat her like that.

It was still weird, having a farm manager not much older than she was. She missed Geai and there was no way Austin had even a fraction of their old manager's experience. Something major had been lacking at the farm since Geai's death. But farm help was hard to find, and sometimes you had to take a chance on someone. It just seemed to work better when Nate and Liv and her parents were around.

But Nate and Liv would soon leave for Florida. Her parents were in Montreal with her father's recently widowed mother. A few weeks ago, they'd announced they were moving back there after twelve years in Ontario, though Emilie was expecting them for Christmas. Her parents, at least. She already knew Liv and Nate wouldn't be here.

She wasn't sure she wanted to be the one in charge of overseeing things on the family's Thoroughbred breeding farm, however temporary that post was. Not that she didn't appreciate their trust. She was only twenty-three, younger than Liv by four years. *Everyone thinks you're so mature, but are you really?* When Liv had pressed her, though, she'd told her sister to go. *Go, ride horses all winter in Florida like you always do. Go start your new life with Nate. I've got this.* Emilie was stalwart. Everyone could count on Em.

That wasn't entirely fair to Liv. Extenuating circumstances meant Liv was sharing training duties this winter — another temporary arrangement, while their regular trainer took a leave of absence because of his wife's illness. But that aligned with Liv's future. Emilie loved the farm, but it wasn't going to be her career. She had a different future planned out. Sort of. Mostly.

The steady sound of munching eased away her tension, the circles she made against Reba's thick orange coat with the rubber curry comb augmenting the effect. Wax on, wax off. Reba didn't budge, nosing through her hay, her pink lips finding the most choice bits first. She wouldn't miss a single alfalfa leaf. It was important for a racehorse to have a healthy appetite. Running required a lot of energy. Reba had mastered that skill, though as a result, the two-year-old's barrel didn't look very racehorse-like — even though she'd been galloping steadily for nearly two months now.

"We'll show them, won't we?" Emilie whispered,

exchanging the curry for a pair of dandy brushes, re-ordering Reba's fuzzy chestnut coat with quick flicks of her right hand. Occasionally, she dragged one brush through the other to clear away the dust.

"All right, sweet pea. That's it for today." Emilie ran a hand down Reba's shoulder.

Reba lifted her head from the pile, turning her face with its wide, irregular blaze and snuffling against Emilie's pocket. Emilie produced the necessary peppermint and gave Reba's soft white nose a quick kiss before ducking out of the stall.

"See ya, Austin!" she called, relieved he wasn't in the tack room when she returned the grooming kit. She didn't wait to figure out where his response came from, shuffling quickly out of the barn and hopping into her car to get out of there before the staff started to arrive. Otherwise, someone would start chatting with her, and she'd be late.

Not bothering to stop by the house to change, she drove out the farm's lane under the tall, skeletal maples. If Faye wasn't used to smelly horse people by now, that was too bad for her. It wasn't as if Emilie had been mucking stalls, anyway. Just one quick ride, doing barely enough to keep both her and Reba warm in December's chilly pre-dawn air. She wasn't even sweaty.

When she reached the parking lot in front of the Triple Shot Café, she squirmed out of her jacket and snow pants and winter paddock boots. She'd leave the items that had actually come into contact with a horse in the car. The shoes she slipped onto her feet had so far managed not to become barn shoes. Horse girl fact: every pair of boots or shoes, from runners to heels, would, at some point in their lives, see the barn. She almost forgot about her hair, and quickly tossed the cap to the side, ran a brush through it and braided it into a single dark plait.

The front window of the café cast a cheery, warm glow into the parking lot. Will — Faye's partner, in business, and in life, it seemed fair to say — had put up bright festive lights around the entrance and the illuminated sign that extended the width of the unit. Fake snow adorned the front window. The bell on the door jingled as Emilie slipped inside. She stood on the doormat for a moment and breathed deep the most wonderful scents in the world — coffee and baking — trying to identify what Faye had in the oven. It wasn't the caramelly amazingness of butter tarts. Ginger chocolate chip muffins, she decided. *Smells like breakfast.*

Evergreen garlands adorned with shiny ornaments decorated the seating area, and now and then she isolated a whiff of pine apart from the food. Faye hadn't deemed a tree necessary, trying to be somewhat generic, out of courtesy for patrons who might not celebrate Christmas.

Emilie did, though. Emilie loved Christmas, and the seasonal decor heightened the wave of happiness that welled up. For a moment she let herself forget those earlier tinges of sadness for what it wouldn't be, this time around.

Faye's head poked out from the kitchen, her dark hair controlled neatly in a bun. "Emilie! Let me start your cappuccino."

Emilie dragged her shoes over the mat and, once satisfied she wasn't going to leave wet footprints over Triple Shot's still-clean floor, she ventured over to the counter. It didn't matter that the tiles would be muddied and mopped several times throughout the day. The fresh layer of snow was pretty now, but once the temperature warmed up with daylight, everything would get slushy, all of it messy and grey.

"I still can't believe you've become a morning person." She watched her friend tamp the fragrant dark grounds into the stainless steel filter.

"I haven't," Faye said wryly. "Don't be fooled."

While Faye steamed the milk — which made conversation difficult — Emilie wandered, her eyes roaming over the paintings on the walls. She'd curated the show of local art herself, selecting snow and seasonal themes. Together, she and Faye had transformed the cosy café for the holidays. Thank goodness for this, right now. For this space. For Faye. For a little bit of normal in the presently peculiar state of her life.

The white stoneware cup Faye handed her was hot in hands still cold from the barn. She savoured the first cautious sip. Her stomach rumbled so loudly Faye's perfect eyebrows peaked over her brown eyes.

"No breakfast," Emilie apologized. "I can't eat before I ride."

"It just so happens I can fix that for you. Not that you need an invitation, but help yourself."

The ginger chocolate chip muffin went perfectly with the cappuccino, convincing her stomach to quiet down. She wasn't cold anymore. After inhaling the muffin while Faye continued to bustle around, she set her cup to the side and pressed her hands together.

"Put me to work," she said, then didn't wait for Faye's direction, because she helped enough she knew what needed to be done.

Faye drew a tray of butter tarts from the oven, closing her eyes and inhaling the rich aromas that escaped with it. "That smell never gets old. I've almost convinced myself it's as satisfying as eating."

"Almost, but not quite." Emilie laughed.

Faye set the pan on a cooling rack and slid off her oven mitts. "I haven't talked to Liv for a few days. We have to get together to finalize the wedding plans. I can't believe it's just a week away."

"It's the event of the century." Emilie loved weddings almost as much as she loved Christmas. Believed in happily ever after and Hallmark. Even for her sister, who had always dismissed those concepts as thoroughly as Emilie clung to them.

"On par with a royal wedding," Faye agreed. They'd both had doubts Nate and Liv would ever get themselves sorted out, but those two had finally concluded what everyone else had long ago. They were destined to be together — though the rollercoaster that had been their relationship might not resemble the fairytale status Emilie had once assigned it.

"I can do lunch with you and Liv tomorrow. Would that work? Here, of course."

"Perfect," Faye said. "That's soon enough. I don't need to write it down, right?"

Maybe so, but Emilie tapped it into her phone's calendar, anyway. "Is Dean coming? To the wedding, I mean," Emilie asked. Dean, Faye's racehorse-trainer brother, lived with Faye on the farm just down from her own family's Triple Stripe.

"Yes. Stacy can handle being on her own for a couple of days. She's got a friend who's going to stay with her to help out."

"That's nice. I feel bad leaving Austin."

Faye snorted. "Why? He's got people to do the actual work for him."

"You're right." The farm wouldn't fall into ruin in three days. "How are we getting to the airport?"

"Dean's booked one of those airport services. Split between four of us, it's reasonable."

"Good job, Dean." Emilie nodded, then broke into a grin. "We're going to have so much fun."

Faye eyeballed her. "And you're finally going to meet Tim."

Emilie's flush beat out the roll of her eyes, and when a

snappy response failed her, she just smiled with a little laugh. Ever since they'd learned Nate had a younger brother, he'd been pegged as hers. Of course, right? She could go along with it. At Nate and Liv's wedding, she'd be bridesmaid to his groomsman. Sounded like the perfect setup for a good story, as unlikely and impractical as the reality of it was.

She stayed long enough to help Faye through the busiest hours; taking orders, helping fill them, cleaning up. When they hit the mid-morning lull, she removed her apron and reached for her coat.

"Off to the clinic now!"

"Who knew Liv and Nate had to get married in Florida for you to take a few days off?" Faye quipped. "You're going to burn yourself out."

"Oh! I need to take Austin a butter tart. I promised him one for doing my tack this morning," she said, ducking Faye's assertion.

Faye stopped, crossing her arms, and Emilie could tell what she was thinking. "That's very thoughtful of you. I didn't think you liked him."

Emilie sighed. "I don't. Why is it that I'm afraid that I might regret such a small, friendly gesture?" Especially because he probably got one of the farm staff to clean the tack.

"Because, boys?" Faye smirked.

"Why does it take so long for them to grow up and become men?" It literally had to do with their brain development. She knew that maybe not-so-random fact, thanks to too many years of university. It still didn't seem like an acceptable excuse.

"Go." Faye shooed her toward the door. "Too many hard questions. I've reached my quota of clever answers."

"I'm disappointed in you, Faye. I expect more." Emilie's lips tipped up at one end. "Love has made you soft."

Faye's mouth opened, then closed. She finally shrugged with a little smile, not even trying to protest.

What was this world coming to?

Everyone was growing up. Liv and Nate were getting married; Faye had a burgeoning business and solid romantic connection with Will. Emilie could be next. It could be with Tim. Why not? If there was a spark, she'd run with it — unlike her sister, who had taken literally years to figure out she should not let the great love that was Nate Miller get away.

She shrugged on her coat, slipping out the door with a wave. She had just enough time to walk down the street to the physiotherapy clinic, change there, and be ready for her first appointment.

As she pulled her bag from the back seat, her phone started ringing. She glanced at the screen — her parents. That returned a smile to her face, and after slinging her bag over her shoulder, she locked the car and answered, pressing the phone to her ear as she strode across the parking lot.

Her mind adjusted to her mother's French, switching like a circuit. It was weird that she herself so rarely spoke it anymore — really only with her parents — when it had been her first language; all she'd spoken for eleven years.

"How are things going, Emilie?"

"Great!" she answered, nearly believing it was true. She wouldn't say otherwise to her mother, anyway. Emilie didn't want her to worry.

"Excited about the wedding?"

"I am. Probably more than the one actually getting married."

Her mother chuckled softly. "We'll be seeing you soon, then."

"How is Papa's mother?"

"She's not well, unfortunately. That's why I'm calling. It

doesn't look as if we'll be coming back for Christmas after all. We'd thought we'd bring her with us, but she's not up to making the trip and your father has agreed to spend Christmas with her. They've been talking. There's been some reconciliation."

"Oh — well... that's good." She didn't sound convincing, least of all to herself. "I'm glad for them. But I'm sad you won't be coming."

"You could come here, Emilie. That would be nice. It would be good for you to get to know your grandmother. And you shouldn't be alone for Christmas."

She hesitated. "I'll have to talk to Austin." The wedding would be a good trial run, but feeling she needed to babysit him — when he'd been the manager since September — seemed a handy excuse not to go. But her mother was right. Christmas was no time to be alone.

CHAPTER 2

The house was dark when she got home from the clinic. It was depressingly devoid of decorations, the only thing remotely related to Christmas being the poinsettia her physiotherapist boss, Sam, had given her last week. Her sister was useless in the holiday cheer department. To be fair, Liv was never around for the decorating part. She was usually in Florida by now, leaving mid-November with the racehorses.

This year Liv's engagement to Nate had apparently inspired her to stay until this weekend's end to the race meet, but she hadn't miraculously suggested they get a tree and pull out the tinsel. You'd think she could've come up with a little Christmas spirit, seeing as the family would be apart this year. Emilie couldn't quite wrap her head around her parents spending the holidays with members of a family she'd never really known. She hadn't decided if she would make the trip to Montreal, when Liv most definitely would not be there. She and Nate were going to Calgary to spend the holiday with his family. But the alternative was being here. Alone. Sure, Faye and Dean would invite her over, but that wasn't the same as people being home, filling the house, giving it life.

She hung her coat in the closet and flicked on the outside lights — token strands of Christmas colours that remained in place year-round because they were so hard to put up. She'd have to remember to hang the wreaths on the door, and the gate by the road. Where was the box they were in? Somewhere in the basement, or the garage. Maybe after dinner, she'd look for them.

Nate had promised to make her and Liv dinner one night before they left for Florida, and tonight was supposed to be that night, but Liv had texted half an hour ago apologizing profusely that he wasn't going to manage it after all. Emilie accepted the disappointment with her usual grace, because that's what she always did. Getting upset just wasn't worth the effort.

Gazing into the fridge was a reminder they needed groceries — another thing Liv was hopeless at. The sooner she married Nate, the better. He knew how to feed himself at least, and would cook for her. How had Liv landed this guy again? If his brother was like that, she definitely needed to open that door.

She opted for a Tetra Pak of soup, emptying part of it into a saucepan to heat on the stove and putting the rest in the fridge. Half a bottle of wine rested on the counter, so she poured herself a glass and sipped, stirring the soup.

There was a stack of unopened Christmas cards piled on the dining room table — which these days wasn't used for anything more than a place to put mail she needed to forward to her parents. Things that had slipped through the address change at the post office. She'd opened the ones addressed to her; there were only a handful of them, because how many people her age sent cards? Liv had to be reminded about any that came for her, at least twice, before they joined Emilie's. The folded greetings sat in a neat row on the buffet at the end of the room, behind the table and under a large painting of a snowy scene on a sunny day, two alert horses looking off into the distance. She loved that her parents decorated with an equine theme — and that they hadn't taken her favourite pieces with them.

The sound of the front door opening made her jump until she realized it was Liv. In a few moments, her sister appeared in the kitchen. Her cheeks were flushed from being out in the cold.

"Hey," Emilie said. "Where were you?"

"Just checking on the girls."

The girls being Chique and Claire. Chique was a four-year-old filly who had recently retired from racing after a successful career, and Claire, now six, was a former star racemare, due to have her first foal in January. Claire was Liv's heart horse, with Chique running a close second. She'd probably have a harder time leaving them behind than anything — or anyone — else.

"Annnnnnd, Nate?" Emilie grinned. A safe bet, especially as he lived in the apartment over the barn the girls were in.

Liv smiled demurely. "Duh."

"He'd better have a good excuse for backing out on dinner," Emilie chided.

Liv shrugged elusively. "He was just heading out. Probably top-secret last-minute Christmas shopping." If she knew his reason for standing them up, she wasn't sharing.

"Do you want some soup?" Emilie asked. "I can heat up the rest."

"Sure. It's the least I can do after Nate bailing," Liv said. "Thanks Em."

Liv set out cutlery on the kitchen table while Emilie

divided the soup between two bowls once it was warm. It felt a little homey, this rare shared meal with her sister.

"Wine?" she asked.

Liv accepted the glass and slipped into the kitchen nook.

"Everything set to go?" Emilie settled across from her. "You sure are packing a lot into the next week. Running Jay on Sunday, leaving for Florida Monday, getting married on Thursday."

"It's just a week. The last while has been pretty laid back, with only Jay at the track. The backstretch is practically empty. It was nice of Dean to offer us a stall for Jay in his barn. Our shed is deserted. Poor Jay would have been all on his own."

"I guess Dean's not going on his usual post-season vacation this year if he's coming to the wedding."

"I guess not," Liv agreed, her eyes dropping as she dipped her spoon into the bisque. "I'm glad he's coming. I was worried he wouldn't."

Dean had always kept his love life to himself — if he even had one — so it had shocked Emilie when he'd come out professing feelings for Liv at the track's biggest social event of the year. He and Liv had always been good friends, but only Faye had suspected her brother wished there was more to their relationship. Emilie didn't know what he'd been thinking. Not that Nate and Liv had been a sure thing at that point, but they were inevitable. Emilie imagined Dean doing something crazy, like standing up at the wedding at that point when the minister asked if anyone had any objections to the marriage. Maybe that's why he was going. One last chance to change fate.

"I think he's accepted his lot," she said, not about to express her wild thoughts out loud, least of all to her sister. "He couldn't compete with the fairytale."

What started as a long-suffering expression on her sister's face transitioned into a real smile. "I'll take the fairytale."

"It's about time." Emilie grinned.

"Proof anything is possible, right?"

They both laughed.

"Is there anything I can do for you before you go?" Emilie asked.

"Because you have too much time? I think I should be asking you that question. You're making me feel lazy these days. Just try not to run yourself down before the wedding, okay? I want you there, too."

"I'd have to be in a coma to miss it, don't worry."

What she really wanted at this exact moment was for her parents to come home. For the four of them to get together on Sunday afternoon to find a tree, then decorate it with cheesy Christmas tunes playing in the background as they drank hot mulled cider and ate sugar cookies. But her parents weren't coming home, and Nate and Liv would be busy at the races on Sunday.

There probably wouldn't be a tree this year, unless she went out and cut it herself. She'd seen the perfect one on a hack last weekend with Reba. She'd even tied a piece of blue baler twine around it so she could find it again. But time was running out, so that seemed very unlikely.

"Did Faye text you?" Emilie asked. "We have to get together one last time, right?"

"I thought that's why I put you two in charge of the wedding plans. So I didn't have to do anything." Liv gave her a wry grin.

"If you hadn't decided to have a destination wedding, we'd have happily managed every last detail."

"Florida is not a destination. It's where I spend four months of the year. Every year."

16

Emilie shook her head and sipped her wine.

"And yes, we're on for lunch tomorrow," Liv said. "I have all the time in the world right now compared to you two."

When a sharp rap came on the sliding glass doors that opened to the backyard, Emilie startled for the second time that evening. She wasn't used to being this jumpy in her own home and wished Nate had moved in already, though that wouldn't change the fact that he and Liv would be gone in a few days. She scrambled to her feet and rushed to the living room. And there he was, letting in a whoosh of sub-zero air as he slid the doors open.

"The front door get old? You scared me half to death," she said once she recovered from his dramatic entrance. She glanced at Liv, who seemed unperturbed by her fiancé's unexpected appearance. She was smiling. Conspiratorially, even. "What's going on?"

"Give me a hand, Liv?" Nate said, and Liv brushed past Emilie to help him drag in, then set upright, a spruce tree only as tall as he was. Emilie saw the piece of blue twine tied around one branch. He'd found her tree.

"Oh, Nate! You're the best!" she hurtled herself at him, and he caught her, laughing.

"Let's go find the decorations," Liv said.

Emilie stepped away from Nate, not daring to hope her sister meant that. "Don't you two need to sleep?"

"We only have one horse, and he's in Dean's barn. If we need an extra hour, I'll text him and let him know we'll be a little late." Liv met Emilie's eyes. "This is important."

Emilie blinked away the tears that welled and squeezed Liv. "Thank you."

She was impressed Liv knew where the decorations were: nestled in a corner of the double garage next to a set of winter tires Liv hadn't used in four winters. Liv handed her one of the labelled boxes, lifting the other and following Emilie back to the living room.

Maybe there was no mulled cider or sugar cookies, but this was amazing. Nate had even cued up some Christmas music, which was quite a sacrifice, because it was no secret he hated holiday songs. Emilie pulled out three wreaths and set them to the side — one for the front door, two for the farm gate. Then she drew out a long, silver garland.

"Where's the tinsel?" Nate asked, coming over and peering into the box. "Tinsel before garland."

"No way!" Emilie insisted. "Garland before tinsel. And seeing as you don't live here, I outrank you."

"You're both wrong," Liv interrupted. "Lights first." She pulled a string of bulbs from the other box.

"She's right," Emilie said. She looked at Liv with a slight tilt of her head. "How are you right?"

"Just because I haven't been around for a few years doesn't mean I don't remember, Em."

After Liv strung the lights, all the bulbs a classic white, Emilie plugged them in. She wound the garland around the tree, careful to make her loops symmetrical. Nate distributed the strands of tinsel more randomly. Then they took turns finding spots for the assorted ornaments. Some were old; some were newer. There wasn't room for all of them because the tree was so small, but Emilie made sure each of her favourites was there.

"Don't forget the star," Emilie said.

Liv pulled it from the box and handed it to Nate. "Do the honours?"

"My pleasure," he said.

That was the plus of a pint-sized tree: all he had to do was set it on the middle stem. The lights caught its faceted gold surface, and when Nate turned off the lamps in the living room, reflections scattered on the walls and high ceiling.

"It's beautiful," Emilie sighed.

Liv shuffled away to the front foyer and returned with a bag. She withdrew a wrapped box and held it out. "Here."

"But... I haven't got you two anything! I've been so busy, and —"

"No worries, Em," Nate said. "We know."

"And I get Nate," Liv said, and grinned as she wrapped an arm around his neck and kissed him on the cheek.

"Awww," Emilie said. "I don't know who you are and what you've done with my sister, but that's sweet."

"Open it," Liv urged.

The box had weight to it, and she kept herself from shaking it, just in case. She sat on the couch and set the present on the coffee table. The bow was a stick-on one, and she pulled it off, then began scraping away the tape.

"Are you really one of those people?" Nate said, looking impatient. "Just tear the damn paper. You can recycle it just as easily that way."

"Now I know it bugs you, no. I won't." She grinned at him and continued with painfully slow progress. Even so, it didn't take long to remove the foil wrapping and reveal a Canon DSLR camera with a short lens.

"Oh, wow!" she said, staring at the box. This was no cheap gift. "Thank you!"

"You realize it's for Liv as much as you, right?" Nate said. "It's so you can take great photos of Claire's foal while we're away. Which is why you need this, too." He produced another box from the bag, about the same size, but heavier. It was in a gift sack instead of wrapped.

She tugged open the drawstring at the top and drew out a telephoto lens. "That's incredible! I'm going to have so much fun. It'll be my pleasure to take those pics. Thank you both so much." She hugged each of them, her eyes damp again. "I'm going to miss you both so much."

"We'll see you next week," Liv reminded.

"I know," Emilie responded. And her parents would be there too. It would be wonderful. But it wouldn't be Christmas.

CHAPTER 3

S he hated being late.

Liv was usually the late one, because she didn't like arriving first at a restaurant, but they were meeting at the café so the same rules didn't apply. Faye was so busy right now; this way she didn't have to leave work. Emilie was happy for a chance to escape the clinic. Not that she hated it, she just welcomed a break when she worked the whole day.

"Hi Lucy!" Emilie called as she wiped her feet on the door-mat, taking a moment to inhale, as she always did. Scones, maybe? "How are you?"

The hobbit-like middle-aged woman behind the counter gave her a smile — something Emilie would never have expected in the days when Lucy had operated the café. Her dark curls were longer and softer now. The lines on her face remained, but had adopted a more relaxed pattern.

"I'm hanging in there, Emilie. I really miss this place. It's nice to come back for a bit. What will you have?"

Faye and Liv were already at a table in the corner, fingers on the handles of white cups set on saucers.

"Are there any of the little quiche left?" Emilie didn't see them in the display.

"Faye stashed a few in the back for the three of you. Spinach and feta."

"Perfect. I can make my own cappuccino."

"No, no." Lucy waved her away. "I can manage. I wasn't sure about that fancy machine at first, but I've come around. Go sit."

"Thanks Lucy!"

Emilie shrugged out of her coat and draped it over the back of the unoccupied chair when she reached the table. She slipped into her seat. "It's nice to have her back. Lucy, I mean."

"She saved the day for me," Faye said, taking a sip from her cup. "If she hadn't agreed to cover for me, I wouldn't be going to the wedding."

"Her mom must be doing okay, then?" Liv asked. The reason Lucy had given up the café last year, Faye taking over, had been to care for her ageing mother.

"Holding her own, I guess," Faye said. "If she's anything like Lucy, she's tough." She raised her eyes, the words trailing off as she smiled, Lucy approaching with Emilie's cappuccino.

"Here you go," Lucy said, placing the cup in front of her. "You've done a wonderful job decorating the place. Faye tells me you had a lot to do with that, Emilie."

"I can't take all the credit," Emilie insisted, thinking how much Lucy had mellowed. "It was a group effort."

"I was not part of that group," Liv said, her lips twisting sheepishly.

Emilie laughed, reaching for the cup. "You redeemed yourself last night."

"I'll be back in a minute with your quiches," Lucy said, leaving them again.

They discussed what they needed to about the wedding

while they ate lunch, Liv happy to let Faye and Emilie manage most of it, though the ultimate concept had been all hers. She would act as courier for their outfits, because she and Nate were driving the farm truck and trailer to Florida. It would let Faye and Emilie travel light on the plane.

"Have you started your dog search yet, Em?" Liv asked, clearly more comfortable with that subject.

"Just checking out websites so far. Rescue groups and such."

"You're getting a dog?" Faye said, her eyebrows arching as she smiled. "That's long overdue."

"So I'm not crazy, with my schedule?"

"You'll make it work. And I know you probably think you want a rescue, but that's a tricky business these days. You should call a few breeders," Faye suggested. "I know Gus's breeder often has older dogs that come back for one reason or another, or they retire the females after a certain number of litters. They're always looking for good homes. I could email her for you and see if she has anything."

"Would you?" Emilie didn't care about breed. Gus was wonderful, all goofy Golden Retriever personality and hair. Lots and lots of hair. Would she even need a boyfriend if she had a dog as great as Gus? "Do they have puppies right now?"

"They do. I really should unfollow their Facebook page, because they are far too cute, and I am much too tempted."

"Gus needs a baby sister," Emilie insisted.

"Enabler," Faye scolded.

"I thought you didn't want a puppy," Liv interjected.

"I don't," Emilie said, then grinned. "But there's nothing wrong with getting a fix. Want to come?"

Liv laughed. "Tempting, but unlikely I could fit it in before I leave — which is probably for the best. I'll expect pictures, though."

Pictures were what this relationship would live on soon. Liv would want daily updates on Claire while she was away, and Emilie was an Instagram addict, anyway. She was excited about her new camera. Her feed was going to get an upgrade.

She managed the farm account as well as her own personal account. The farm one wasn't so much a business thing — the Lachance family's Triple Stripe Stud wasn't a big operation by Thoroughbred racing standards — but she liked to showcase it; give people a glimpse into what went on, in some vain hope the public would feel a personal connection to a world they all too often dismissed as being purely about money. If they only knew how few people actually made any in that sport.

"Think you'll make it to the races Sunday?" Liv eyed Emilie as she sipped her cappuccino.

Closing day. Liv's expression was hopeful, and Emilie felt bad for not having a definitive answer. "I hope so. It would be a great chance to break out the new DSLR."

It was Just Jay's comeback race. The four-year-old colt had been hanging out in a paddock on the farm, getting fat, since recovering from a hairline fracture in the spring. He was well bred and had done all right on the track, but his career kept getting interrupted by bad-luck injuries, and four was, insanely, considered old for a racehorse. Emilie had started riding him over the summer to give him something to do while her father and sister decided if he was going to be sold as a stallion prospect to who knows where, or if they might bring him back to the races. She'd been playing around with low-level dressage and doing conditioning intervals with him when Nate had found out, seen how great the colt looked, and petitioned to put Jay back in training. Triple Stripe's private trainer, Roger Cloutier, had agreed Jay deserved another chance to shine on the track. So did Emilie, albeit reluctantly, because she missed riding the big chestnut. She had Reba now, at least.

Faye remained silent, her eyes on Emilie like she knew her wavering was about something more complicated than scheduling. Because if Emilie said she wanted to go to the races, Faye would say go. She'd manage the work they'd planned at the café on her own — they were just trying to do some prep to make things easier for Lucy while they were away. Emilie tried to pinpoint the reason for her reluctance. She loved the horse. She loved the races. But there was always something sad about the end of the season. It was a goodbye, and this time it seemed a bigger goodbye than other years.

Goodbye to Jay — because if they were successful with him, he had the potential to end up standing at a farm in Kentucky, which might be great, or not so great.

Goodbye to Liv — because she would be gone for the winter, and even though Emilie loved Nate, and loved Nate and Liv together, it still meant more change. It reminded her she was the lone single one in their group. It wouldn't surprise Emilie at all if Will and Faye got engaged soon.

Enough of her morose thoughts. She forked in the last mouthful of quiche and tossed back the rest of her coffee. "I've got to fly. Back to work!"

Work that got in the way. Of her friendships. Of her horses. But she'd decided she would have a career that let her enjoy both on her terms. She would not be like Liv, totally immersed in something that wasn't just a job, or a career — it was a lifestyle. She would have balance. Not that she had any right now.

She dashed down the street to the clinic, grateful it was so close. In her head, she arranged the next few days. Tomorrow — Saturday! She only worked half a day at the clinic, so there was extra time for Reba, and maybe she could go see the puppies if Faye connected with Gus's breeder. Then Sunday, at the café, and maybe the races. Monday, Liv and Nate left with Jay aboard the trailer — unless he ran so poorly on Sunday they deemed his comeback a failure. Emilie couldn't see that happening, though. Jay was born to be a star. This was his time.

Last year Emilie had made that drive to Florida with Liv after Christmas; not hauling a horse, or following the van, but straight through from Erie, Pennsylvania. Twenty-one hours, only stopping for gas and short breaks because of Liv's separation anxiety; her need to get back to Chique and Feste, their next big hopeful. It had been Emilie's first time; an adventure, though the fun had worn off once those hours in the car added up, then taken another ding when they'd arrived at the training centre to find Chique seriously ill.

She didn't envy Liv and Nate that drive, but she was still just a little jealous of them. Of their clear path, when she felt as if her own had too many intersections.

CHAPTER 4

Emilie didn't have to work every Saturday at the clinic, and on the days she did, they were only open until noon, anyway. She was working today because she'd booked next Saturday off — she'd be home, but what fun would it be to jump right back to work after the wedding? See, she was trying to balance her life.

Two weeks from today was Boxing Day; they were in the Christmas home stretch. Most of the patients were in holiday mode, and some even brought cards and treats. It wasn't an unpleasant morning, passing quickly, but she still skipped gleefully to her car once she was done and headed straight to the training barn at the farm. She didn't have to ride in the dark today, woo-hoo! And it was a hack day; a mental health break for both her and Reba.

Quiet munching was the only sound in the dark barn until she passed Reba's stall and was greeted with a low rumble. Reba's blaze stood out against her coat, her head backlit by the window as it popped up. The filly's facial marking looked as if a small moon was in the early stages of an eclipse, creating a perfect half-circle bite of chestnut on one side at eye level.

Reba was content to be in the barn on her own; it was otherwise empty, the nightly inhabitants turned out, stalls already mucked and the staff on their lunch break. Perfect timing. Not that Emilie was antisocial, but it would save her precious minutes if she didn't get caught up in conversation. She was on a mission today. Ride Reba, then a couple of recently retired horses for New Chapter she'd taken on. Then tonight: puppies. The perfect day.

She mounted from the block just outside the barn, and Reba stepped out lightly over the gravelled surface, warm sunlight melting away the remnants of ice on the edges of the lane that led around the farm. The filly was barefoot and didn't seem to miss her aluminum plates; they'd pulled her shoes when she'd returned from the few weeks she'd been at the track this fall. Roger, the trainer, liked the two-year-olds to spend time there, even if they didn't yet show any interest in being a racehorse.

Reba hadn't exactly been what track people called precocious. If she woke up at three, the time she'd spent at Woodbine would serve as her introduction to that life. If she didn't and was destined only to be a riding horse, the bone density she'd built would contribute to her future soundness, and the sights and sounds she'd been exposed to on the backstretch expanded her world and made her a better equine citizen. Not that she wasn't perfect already. Reba, at two, was more bombproof than many older horses she knew. Emilie reached down and scrubbed the filly's neck with her knuckles, smiling as Reba's head dropped a few more degrees, a happy snort fluttering from her nostrils.

The weanling fillies clambered against the fence as she passed; scruffy and feral with unkempt manes and coats wooly from living outdoors. She'd remind Austin before she left for Florida that when she returned, they'd start coming in at night to re-learn the manners they'd lost since being separated from their mothers. Reba's head drifted in their direction, acknowledging them but never missing a step.

It was silent in the woods; the evergreens preserving the snow on the ground. She saw the stump left from her Christmas tree and felt a twisted pang of happy and sad. It was such a nice thing Nate had done; better than any dinner he would've made. She just wished they weren't leaving until after the holiday. Maybe next year.

She turned Reba out afterward and watched as the filly immediately dropped and rolled in the combination of mud and melting snow. Reba rose, shaking, looking quite satisfied with the way she'd marred her bright coat, and wandered over to her pals parked at the hay station.

The crew was returning from lunch as she was in the indoor arena getting on Note To Self, the first of the project horses. She spotted Jillian, one of the workers, watching in the doorway as she walked the gelding on a long rein.

Jillian was tall, in a willowy kind of way. Horse-girl designation: hunter rider. She didn't ride at Triple Stripe, but had figured out Thoroughbred outfits paid better than show barns. Riding was never promised, though it was probably a secret hope of some of the young women who did stints on staff. Time to find out. Jillian might be able to help. Emilie steered Note To Self over.

Jillian reached up and offered her palm to the gelding. "He's such a cutie."

"Do you want to ride him?" Emilie asked.

Jillian looked up at Emilie, eyes bright. "Seriously? I'd love to."

"I'd like to keep him going while I'm away. New Chapter

has a couple of people they want to send to try him before Christmas if I think he's ready. Don't suppose you have your boots and helmet with you?"

Jillian grinned. "Just so happens, I do."

Emilie smiled back at her. Secret revealed. "Great. Is Austin there? I'll tell him I'm going to steal you for half an hour."

She resumed walking on the rail while Jillian was gone, gradually shortening her reins, so when she closed her legs around the gelding, he reached for the bit and began stepping underneath himself nicely. She caught sight of Austin at the door.

"I'll help bring in," she called, hoping to make up for taking away some of his help.

"I think the sacrifice is worth a little more," Austin said, leaning on the top of the door as his eyes followed her. "Like you have to agree to have dinner with me."

Emilie glanced at his sly smile and controlled her expression, putting on what she hoped was a look of regret. "I honestly won't have a spare moment before the wedding," she apologized. "Sorry."

"When you get back, then."

Jillian reappeared at just the right time, getting Emilie out of answering. She halted Note To Self in the centre of the arena and dropped her stirrups. "Come on in, Jillian."

All of Jillian's gear was high-end — her helmet probably cost more than Emilie's entire outfit. Emilie dismounted and waited while Jillian said hello, then adjusted the stirrups, dropping them several holes. Her legs were way longer than Emilie's.

"He's very sensible," Emilie said as Jillian checked the girth, and noticed with relief that Austin was gone. "You can get on using the mounting block. He's really good with it now."

She watched with satisfaction as Jillian rode; the gelding

liking the young woman's soft hands and quiet seat. A few suggestions from Emilie, and Note To Self went as well for Jillian as he did for her.

"I love him!" Jillian called, her grin huge. "Why can't I afford two horses?"

Emilie laughed. "Where there's a will, there's a way, right?"

"I wish," Jillian said, walking Note To Self off the rail toward Emilie. "I'm going to tell a friend of mine about him."

"He'll make a really nice hunter, I think. Tell her to go on New Chapter's website and fill out an application! I call him Selfie." Emilie rubbed the big star in the middle of the gelding's forehead. "You don't mind getting on him while I'm gone? And Quizzical? She's really uncomplicated too. I'll tell Austin, but it might have to be on your own time depending on the day."

Jillian nodded. "I'll even come in on my day off. This is perfect. My guy is off right now — pulled a shoe and bruised his foot, so this way I have something to ride. Thanks, Emilie."

"Thank you! Here, I'll take him. Wouldn't want to keep you from whatever Austin needs you for."

Jillian rolled her eyes. "We only have part of one barn to finish before we bring them in and feed."

Once Selfie was untacked and settled in his stall, she rode Quizzical, then changed back into winter boots and a toque. She zipped on her coat and grabbed a lead shank to begin bringing in the individually turned out horses close to the training barn. Then she joined the others to finish, using Jillian as a shield from Austin by talking about the New Chapter horses.

"I'll bring Claire and Chique in," she said, not stopping long enough to be cornered by the manager, leaving the staff to start feeding.

Claire and Chique were waiting by the gate, the two of them a study in contrasts. Claire was tall, nearly seventeen hands; a bright bay with a wide, jagged blaze that dropped off her face into one of her nostrils. Her roundness from the foal she carried made her all the more massive. Chique was probably six inches smaller, her coat inky-dark, her body maintaining the sleek lines of a racing-fit horse. Her long forelock covered her only white marking, the tiniest of stars on her forehead. Emilie took Claire in first, the big mare nodding placidly next to her. She filled her straw-bedded stall, turning immediately to her hay.

Chique pawed the ground with a forefoot. "Oh, the injustice of being the last one in," Emilie consoled.

Chique power-walked next to her all the way into the barn. She had just enough time to feed the two horses, have a shower, and make it to the breeder for her appointment.

"Are you sure you don't want to come?" she asked Liv, who had miraculously picked up some groceries and was putting them away. Emilie looked around for Nate, sure he must be responsible, but didn't see him.

"I'm still resisting that temptation." Liv grinned at her. "I'm determined to get packed tonight, because I sure don't want to be doing it tomorrow night after the races."

"All right," Emilie said. "I guess that's a good reason."

"Pictures, though!" Liv reminded.

"Definitely."

Last night, thanks to Faye's referral, she'd visited Gus's breeder. The Golden Retriever puppies were adorable; fluffy and Naples Yellow-coloured. They were somehow related to Gus, but Emilie didn't quite catch how. She'd snapped numerous photos with her camera. The DSLR would have been overkill, so she'd left it at home.

"We have a young male, six months old, coming back to us next week. Is that something you'd be interested in? He's a lot of dog — too much for the people who took him. Sometimes, as much care as we put into the process, we don't get the right match."

"Yes, absolutely," Emilie said. "I'm going away for a few days next week, but I'd love to come see him when I'm home again. I don't usually go away at all," she added quickly, not wanting the breeder to think she took off all the time.

"Faye vouched for you. That's enough for me. She and Dean have given Gus a wonderful home. And if you ever do go away, we're happy to board him for you."

"What's his name?"

"Theo."

"I can't wait to meet him."

She imagined Theo and Gus romping as she and Faye walked through the fields at Northwest. She'd probably have to do some training first. Faye would help her. She'd done a good job with Gus. Emilie left there excited. She might have a dog by Christmas. Not that she was getting a dog for Christmas. It just happened to be Christmas, and she'd be getting a dog.

During a break this morning at the clinic she'd found the name of a Labrador breeder, and couldn't resist contacting them, even though the kennel's website had been so old it amazed her it still worked — archaic HTML with tiny photos, though the "news" page was up to date. They also had a litter. She'd called, guessing a breeder like that might take a week to reply to email. No, she wasn't getting a puppy. But she was sure the same thing was true of this one as with Gus's breeder: they might have older dogs in need of a new situation.

It was a whim, an indulgence, that she was going to see them. A little nostalgia for the last two dogs that had lived on the farm, both black Labs: Geai's Napoleon, and her father's Josée, who had been littermates. She turned down the dirt laneway, avoiding potholes, until she reached a house and kennel building. Despite the condition of the lane, the grounds were neatly kept, if dated. A chorus of happy barks greeted her, coming from both the house and the kennel. No doorbell was needed. An older woman, probably in her seventies, waited on the doorstep.

"You must be Emilie. I'm Norma. Come in and meet everyone."

A herd of Labradors — that's the only way she could describe it — clustered politely behind the woman. Until Norma shut the door, that is. Then joyous wriggling Labs swarmed her, every acceptable colour represented. Just beyond them hovered a leggy Greyhound.

"You're not a Labrador." Emilie laughed, feeling silly, but compelled to state the obvious.

"That's Clara," Norma said. "She was a rescue. Lovely girl. You're involved with rescued racehorses, aren't you?"

Emilie nodded, not bothering to correct Norma that the horses she worked with hadn't been rescued from anything. She was too immersed in black and yellow and chocolate bodies.

"Oh — that's Charles, my husband." Norma indicated a man off to the left in the living room, parked in a recliner. He smiled, and Emilie gave him a little wave. "Come and see the puppies first," Norma continued. "Then I'll make some tea. You're wearing a clean change of clothes?"

She nodded again. Norma had asked her to be sure of that, even though she hadn't been around any dogs today. It was protocol Emilie was familiar with on the farm. Biosecurity, essentially. Puppies were as vulnerable to disease as young foals were.

An adoring gasp escaped her when she saw them. They were sweet little black nuggets. Chunky chunks of coal. It was all she could do not to make grabby hands at them.

"We were expecting some Chocolates," Norma explained. "But they're all black. All six of them."

"Black's my favourite colour. I grew up with a Black Labrador. Can I pick one up?"

Norma nodded. "Go right in with them."

Emilie lifted one, a fat little sausage. Smelled the puppy breath. Listened to the endearing little puppy grunts. She decided her next dog would be a puppy. Because there would be another. Down the road, when her life was more settled. Saner. When she got a puppy, she would want all the time in the world to devote to it. So what made her think she could fit in a boyfriend right now? Pretty much the same, wasn't it? Needy. Demanding.

"We're also part of the Labrador Rescue Network," Norma said. "If we get a surrender we think is suitable, we'll let you know. We keep your paperwork on file. We'd just have to do a home visit prior to any placement."

"No problem," Emilie said. "You have my cell, so don't hesitate to call." She almost offered to update the website for them. *Because you have so much free time, Emilie?*

Before she drove off, she texted photos of the tiny black Labs to Liv.

If you smuggle one home, I promise to look the other way, Liv texted back.

Sorry, too young, Emilie replied, and drove home with a smile she defied anyone to wipe from her face.

CHAPTER 5

Wielding the rolling pin with practiced hands, she resisted the temptation to pop a piece of dough into her mouth. It wasn't the raw eggs that made her stop — she'd eaten enough unbaked cookie dough in her life and never suffered a food-borne disease as a result — it just seemed inappropriate when baking for the public. All bets were off in her own kitchen. There was always a spoonful left at the end; she'd wait for that.

"I won't have to do any baking." She wiped a smudge of flour from her nose with the back of her hand and grinned at Faye. Though how much would she need, really? Maybe some for the farm staff. It seemed pointless to take a tin of goodies to Faye and Dean now, which is what she'd always done in the past.

She pressed through the dense dough, cutting the shapes, then freed them from the stainless surface with her lifter, sliding them onto the large cookie pan. Into the oven they went. After setting the timer, she turned to Faye.

"That's it for the sugar cookies. They'll need time to cool before I can decorate them. What should I do next?"

"Can you start the Nanaimo bars?"

"I would love to. A big pan, right?"

Faye nodded. "Can never have enough of them!"

Instrumental holiday music, a playlist supplied by Faye's boyfriend Will, drifted in from the café. Faye couldn't take the constant overplayed vocal versions played just about everywhere you went this time of year. Emilie secretly loved them.

Were Nanaimo bars as Canadian as the butter tarts the café was famous for? They'd inherited that renown from Lucy. People still came in looking for Lucy's butter tarts and were overjoyed to find the recipe lived on even though Lucy had retired. The menu had been bare-bones in those days; the coffee only bearable because of the pastry. Faye and Will had upgraded the place for sure.

Emilie lined up the ingredients for the base of the bars. Cocoa, coconut, vanilla cracker crumbs, butter, vanilla, walnuts. "Wait — there's an egg? I thought these things were no-bake."

"I didn't say that. You just assumed."

She combined the ingredients and pressed them into the pan, then, following the recipe, slipped the pan into the oven after removing the now-baked cookies. While the cookies cooled, she started on the best part: the sweet middle custard layer. Well, it wasn't really custard; more like icing with custard powder in it. She mixed it up and set it aside.

Faye wandered out into the front, and Emilie could see her staring out the door.

"It's snowing pretty good out there," Faye said when she returned. "Are you going to the races this afternoon?" She resumed mixing a batch of gingerbread that would spend the night in the fridge for rolling out and cutting into shapes tomorrow.

Emilie glanced at the time. She'd have to leave now, if the roads weren't likely to be clear, to give herself enough time to get to Woodbine. It would be stupid to drive all that way and miss the race. She should go to watch Jay, though Liv had hired someone to take the colt over for the race, and someone to walk him after, so she didn't need Emilie's help. She looked outside herself.

The flakes were fluffy and fat, and descending at an impressive rate. A good old-fashioned snowfall. A few centimetres had accumulated on her car, and on the ground, and on the trees across the street. It looked as if the decision was made for her.

"I'm just going to stay," she told Faye when she returned to the kitchen. "It really is coming down out there. I'll watch on my phone." She hadn't promised she'd be there. Her sister would understand.

Emilie checked the time. Liv would still be at the barn, getting Jay ready. She'd text and let her know she wasn't coming.

I understand, came Liv's reply, as expected. *Wish you were here, though.*

There was that pang of guilt. Liv didn't say stuff like that often. Closing day had a lonely feel to it, and she'd be watching the race on her own, which would make it worse.

Me too, Emilie responded, though part of her didn't wish it. The part that fought the separation that would follow, as if it would prevent it from happening. *Good luck. I'll be watching.*

"What's next, Faye?" she asked, needing to be busy.

"We're going to have to do some dishes soon. Want to start on that?"

She dove into the task, filling the dishwasher with everything that could go in it, and starting the machine before washing the rest. It wouldn't be long before the base of the Nanaimo bars would be ready to come out of the oven.

The icing, divided and coloured, waited for the sugar cookies. They were cool to the touch, so the next job was to decorate. She loved this part, happily absorbing herself.

"Aren't you going to watch the race?" Faye reminded.

Emilie glanced over her shoulder at the clock on the wall of the kitchen. "Agh! Yes. Thank you. Are you coming?"

Faye dusted flour from her hands and rinsed them off. "Sure. I can still appreciate Nate Miller on a horse. And I can most certainly cheer for my best friend." Faye's comments about Nate — who she'd dated for nine months, before Liv — were light-hearted. That hadn't always been the case. "We can use my laptop. How much time do I have?"

Emilie set the laptop up on a table in the café, deserted on a Sunday afternoon. She clicked on the video feed in time to see the horses just leaving the paddock. "About ten minutes."

"If we're taking a break, we're having cappuccino. It's not too late for you, is it?"

Emilie laughed. "Never!"

It was only snowing lightly at Woodbine. Jay was the picture of composure, Nate looking like his usual relaxed self as he talked with the pony rider. The chestnut colt looked fabulous, like a bronze sculpture, the artificial overhead lights catching the contour of every muscle. She missed him, but this was right. He was meant to be more than her pony. It was time for him to become the racehorse they knew he could be. Now she regretted not making the effort, wishing she could teleport there; be there first hand and not on the other side of a computer screen.

Faye was silent as she slid a cup with its warm, frothy contents across to Emilie, her own mug clasped in her fingers as she sat. Emilie was too nervous to pick hers up. It would need time to cool, anyway.

A mile and three-quarters. It was a long race. But Jay had won it last year, and he looked bigger and stronger than he had then. Fluffy flakes drifted from the dark sky, in no hurry to reach the earth. The field loaded quickly, then they were off.

Without Jay, though. "Oh no," she moaned. He broke a length behind the others. A little too relaxed, maybe?

"That was weird," Faye said. She was here more as moral support than because she really cared. Okay, she cared to the extent that they were all friends, and she didn't want anything to go wrong, but horse racing on the whole had never been her passion. She'd never sat on a racehorse. Never felt that thrill, that power, that heart. Emilie couldn't expect her to understand.

Jay stayed at the back of the pack, getting only the occasional call from the track announcer who described the race's progress. Emilie swallowed the hard lump in her throat. *Come on Jay. You remember what this is about.*

Nate made no attempt to rouse the colt until they had less than a quarter mile to go. Then it was like Jay shifted gears, powering up and taking off. He flew, blowing by his rivals, making them look like Wile E. Coyote when the roadrunner zoomed past — frozen in his dust. Emilie was speechless. She should be on her feet, screaming, but she was transfixed by the jaw-dropping display. One she should have been there in person for.

"Wow!" Faye spoke first. Even she was glued to the screen, staring as Jay continued to roll around the clubhouse turn, far in front of his rivals, even though the race was over.

"He's brilliant," Emilie said, in awe that she had been on that horse. Yes, Jay was where he needed to be.

"Is that Roger?" Faye said, leaning closer to the screen as the groom posed Jay for the win photo.

Em followed suit. "It is! I'm so happy he's there."

Liv hadn't watched alone after all. Emilie closed the laptop and felt it sink in. All of it. That was it then. Liv and Nate were leaving her behind to cope with the farm while they went wherever Jay would lead them. And that was okay, wasn't it?

She threw herself back into baking instead of letting herself think about it too much.

The base for the Nanaimo bars was cool, and she spread the icing over it, then set it in the freezer — that way, the chocolate topping would spread more easily. Faye insisted on a thin, bittersweet layer — not the sweeter ganache most bakeries produced. It all sounded like an unlikely combination, but Emilie had tasted Faye's Nanaimo bars, and they were amazing, so she wasn't going to question it.

They cut best before the chocolate became solid, Faye had warned her. After a brief time in the refrigerator to firm up the topping, she sliced them in the pan with a sharp knife and resisted the temptation to sample her handiwork.

"We should wrap this up, Em," Faye said, her gaze sweeping around the kitchen. "The weather's not going to get any better out there, and we made good progress this afternoon."

As they put things away, Faye set aside a selection of what they'd created and divided it into three.

"One for you, one for me to take home to Dean, and one to give Liv and Nate for the drive tomorrow. Tell Liv to text me when they leave the farm and they can stop and pick up cappuccinos, too."

Emilie hugged her and gathered the plastic-covered styrofoam trays. "Thanks, Faye."

"Thanks to you, we're in good shape. I feel okay about leaving Lucy. Not that I don't think she can handle it."

Emilie wasn't sure she had the same confidence in Austin.

CHAPTER 6

It was dark. She rose in the dark; she trained Reba in the dark; she came home from work in the dark; she slept in the dark. The last item was the only one of all of them that was acceptable. But such was life. In another week or so, the days would start to get longer again, right?

She heard the shower running in the bathroom down the hall. It was five AM, and she didn't need to get up yet, but Liv was preparing to leave, and Emilie wasn't about to miss seeing her and Nate off.

She pulled a sweatshirt over her pyjama top and rubbed the crust out of the corners of her eyes. Then she started calculating, working backwards. She had to be at the clinic at eight today. That meant being done with Reba by seven, so she'd have time to shower. What it came down to was, she wasn't going back to sleep, so she might as well get dressed properly.

Making sure Nate and Liv had Faye's care package and instructions for the other part of it — stopping at Triple Shot on the way to the highway for cappuccinos to go — she made a conscious effort not to get teary as she hugged them both and said goodbye.

"See you on Wednesday," Nate said, grinning.

"Have a safe trip," Emilie replied, and bit her lip, waving as they climbed into the cab of the truck. She jumped into her car and headed to the training barn, the taillights of the four-horse gooseneck in her rearview mirror. Reba would set her mind right.

Tuesday was a repeat of Monday, save for the early morning send-off. Liv had texted her a few times on the drive to Kentucky, where she and Nate had stopped for the night. It was as if Liv finally realized others wanted to know they were safe.

One more sleep! Her checklist was long. So much to do before tomorrow's departure. Why was it so hard to break away for just a couple of days? Why did she get herself in over her head like this? Going away should not have to be a production.

"What's happening with Reba while you're gone?" Austin asked as she rushed into the tack room to deposit the grooming kit after her ride.

"Turn her out!" Sometimes this guy was dense. And she was leaving him in charge. Heaven help them all.

"Easy," he said, holding up both hands. "You have Jillian riding those other two, so I just thought..."

There was no time to explain that galloping a racehorse — even one as placid as Reba — wasn't the same as schooling an OTTB, but it had been unfair to snap. She sighed, tossing him a rueful glance.

"I'm sorry. I'm a little stressed out." She didn't miss the

crooked smile he passed back. *A little?* "You have the vet's number, right? And a backup?"

"Yes, Emilie. Everything is going to be okay."

Would it, though? Thank goodness she could rely on the farm staff, because she still wasn't sure about Austin. Call it a gut feeling. It was unfortunate all the people she'd normally rely on were going to be gone, too. Nate and Liv went without saying. Faye and Will. Dean. Everyone already in Florida — Jo, Cory, Nicole; Sue and Michel, all of whom worked with the track horses. She scribbled a few more notes in the book she was leaving for him.

"I'm sure I'm forgetting something."

"You can always text me," he said. "It really will be fine."

Was his hand on her shoulder? She turned her head slightly, saw his fingers there, and moved away. She couldn't afford to make him mad, not now. She needed him. "We'll talk again before I leave, 'k? Read over my notes and let me know if you have questions. Gotta go to the clinic."

He smirked as she left, and she hid her glower. He probably had no intention of reading her carefully written book of Things He Needed To Know.

She jogged to her car, not waiting for it to warm up to drive to the house. A shower was a necessity, because at the clinic they weren't as accepting of traces of horse scent as Faye was, though she did sometimes go there straight from the barn. The scrubs she had to wear always made her feel funny, as if she were masquerading as a doctor. She could have been a doctor. Likely if her parents had gotten things their way, she would have been, and Liv would have been a vet, of course — she'd been only a year away from getting her DVM when she'd dropped out to get her jockey's license. At least, unlike Liv, she would finish her second degree. She had to, even if it wasn't an MD.

Wasn't the youngest child supposed to be the one who gave up the logical path and chased her dreams? Some days... some days she felt like her older sister had stolen that from her. Like because Liv had done it, she'd taken that option away. Because they both couldn't completely disregard the responsibility, could they? Even Nate had commented, once: *One of you girls better stay in school.* He was joking, but...

University wasn't cheap. She shuddered to think of the thousands of dollars her parents had put out for tuition and textbooks. She wondered if Liv ever thought about it. Though Emilie supposed training Chique, who had made over a million dollars in her career, had reimbursed them. Would Chique have won those races with or without Liv?

Her hair was still wet as she brushed it, slicking it into a neat bun. She shrugged into a cardigan and skipped downstairs. There was a knock on the door as she put together snacks — some fruit, a protein bar, a snack-size yogurt, her water bottle. She wasn't expecting anyone, especially this early. Very few people just showed up at the house. Running to the front foyer, she swung open the door.

"Sylvie!" After a split-second to get over the surprise, she threw her arms around the tall young woman on the step. "I'm so sorry. I'm on my way out, but come in for a few minutes while I get my shit together." Literally, not figuratively. That would take much, much longer.

She tried to recall the last time she'd seen the trainer Roger Cloutier's daughter as she took Sylvie's coat and hung it up, then led the way to the kitchen.

"Sorry for being a terrible hostess." She glanced over her shoulder.

"Don't worry about it," Sylvie said. "I should have called first. This was kind of a whim."

"How are you? How's your mom doing?" One question at a

time would be good, Emilie. "When did you get here? How did you get here?" So much for that.

Sylvie laughed. "Saturday. I flew. And I don't know how I am, to be honest. And my mom is my mom. 'Oh, don't worry about me. I'm going to be just fine.'"

Emilie's face fell. "Cancer sucks, so much. I wish I didn't have to go to work right now. Are you free later? Can you come over again then? I'm done at six." That would work. Except for the fact she hadn't packed. She could sleep on the plane.

"I'll check with my parents and let you know?"

"Okay! I'm really so sorry I have to dash. Let me give you my number." She stopped long enough to dictate the sequence, and made Sylvie send her a text, so she had her number, too.

"If I can't make it later, we'll do it when you get back from the wedding."

"I wish you were coming!"

"Me too. But it just wouldn't feel right, you know?"

"I know. All of it sucks." She scooped up her bag of snacks and ushered Sylvie to the front door. They hugged again. "We'll catch up soon either way, okay? But I really hope you can come over tonight."

Sylvie squeezed her shoulders with one arm, clutching her coat in the other. "Me too."

She let Sylvie head out first, and followed the red SUV out the laneway, Sylvie driving more slowly than she would have. Which was good; it forced her to regroup. Austin had the drive cleared, and she felt bad again for snapping at him. He would have been up extra-early to do that and feed the horses. Everything would be all right when she was gone. It wasn't as if she did anything around here but worry about it all. She flashed her lights at Sylvie as she turned one way at the end of the lane, and Sylvie went the other.

Piles of snow bordered the parking lot of the physiotherapy

clinic. The door shut with an efficient click behind her as she stepped inside, wiping her boots on the mat before removing them. She padded in with sock feet, giving the receptionist slash office manager, Trudy, a cautious smile as she slipped past to the staff room. The patients waiting didn't pay her any attention, but Emilie was sure Trudy was judging, judging, judging. She wasn't late, but Trudy was one of those people who was always annoyingly early.

After fishing her most comfortable running shoes from her bag and tugging them on, not bothering to unlace them, she tucked her snacks in the fridge and left her coat hanging on the back of a chair. That drove Trudy nuts. Emilie would cling to that small bit of defiance, but it was mildly pathetic that was as rebellious as she got. Others her age smoked pot and drank excessively. She refused to use the coat rack.

Conversely, Sam, her boss, the physiotherapist who owned the clinic, was easy-going and nice. Emilie got along well with her and valued her as a mentor. Emilie nodded at her as she slithered past Sam's office to the area she'd work with her first patient. Somehow she actually had five minutes to breathe, so she'd made up time somewhere. *Win.*

She took a moment to close her eyes and breathe. Inhale, deeply; exhale, pushing all the air out so her shoulders dropped, tension released — for the most part. Behind her eyes, she saw Reba's bright chestnut ears so vividly she could smell the filly's wonderfully horsey smell, and wondered for a moment if she'd somehow tracked some of it with her. It was a disappointment when she remembered this was just her grounding exercise. Reba was her happy place right now, her port in the storm she always felt was swirling around her.

"All right," she said to the walls as she stood, ready to do what she was here to do, the horsey smell dissipating with the vision. "This is what you want to do with your life, Emilie." A nice inside job, where she could stay clean and dry and not smell like a barn.

She loved that smell, though.

Sam left her on her own for some of the simple cases and invited her in on others where she could learn something. Sam was an excellent teacher, patient when Emilie compared something to horses, though Sam often reminded her of that tendency because not all patients appreciated it. The cases that interested her most were injuries she could relate to. Messed up knees. Back pain. Exercises she could take home and share — or could have shared, when Nate was around. He'd hurt his back seriously this past summer in a riding accident.

Her favourite part was working with kinesiology tape. It was the one thing she brought to the practice; something she'd researched and pursued on her own. She loved seeing patients' expressions transform as they realized they felt better and wondered how it was possible. Emilie explained the idea behind it, but it still always felt kind of magical. The only thing wrong was that they didn't make it with holiday patterns. Really, they needed to do something about that. Of course, as she applied it to humans, she was always thinking about how she could use it for the horses.

It was a relief when the time flew by, and also a reminder she didn't hate this job. She just hated that she spent the best part of the day — daylight hours — inside, in this clinic. She enjoyed the work. It was interesting, and when people actually listened to her and did their exercises, it was rewarding. Could she petition for evening appointments? Maybe Sam and Trudy didn't want to do them because they had families, but Emilie would gladly be available for those times. Especially this time of year, when darkness descended so early. If they offered her a job when she graduated, maybe that was something Sam would consider.

The excitement crept back as the clock ticked closer to six. Then she'd be out of here, and tomorrow, out of Ontario. It would be strange to be in Florida a week before Christmas, but a wedding on the beach was a worthwhile side trip from the seasonal festivities. Christmas would be waiting when she got back.

"Have a wonderful time," Sam said, the sentiment genuine. Even Trudy seemed sincere in her well-wishes for the bride and groom.

"Thanks!" Emilie said, and with a fresh injection of energy, bounced out the door.

Darkness had fallen like a heavy blanket and there was a bite to the air — colder than last night. She started her Honda and checked her texts while it warmed up. One from Faye: *Airport shuttle coming at 6am to our place. Don't be late!* As if. And one from Sylvie: *Invite still good for tonight? I can be there at 7. I'll bring dinner.* Emilie responded quickly. *YES! And I'll supply the wine.*

The lights were still on when she drove past the café, but she didn't stop. She'd see Faye in the morning. In ten minutes, she was home. As soon as her boots were off, she flicked on the coloured outdoor lights, then lit up the Christmas tree in the living room. It helped balance the cavernous emptiness the house had with no one else around. She switched on a few lamps, opened the wine, and dashed upstairs to change into sweats.

Sylvie arrived right on time, presenting Emilie with a casserole dish. "Dinner."

"That's not takeout." Emilie grinned, expecting something in bags and cartons, not what looked to be lasagna.

"My mother insisted I bring it." Sylvie slipped off her shoes and hung her coat in the closet. "They have a freezer full of casseroles. It's what people do when you're sick, apparently. Bring you food you probably don't feel well enough to eat."

Emilie wasn't sure whether to laugh or cry.

The glass dish felt warm; obviously pre-heated. Sylvie followed her to the kitchen, and she turned on the oven to heat it up. "Shall I pour the wine?"

"Please."

The kitchen table was cosier than the alternative — the dining room. It would have been nice to sit in the living room with the tree, but the thought of her mother's face as they balanced plates of lasagna on their laps while seated on that pristine cream sofa forced her to banish that idea.

The table in the kitchen was nestled into an alcove with a bench on either side. Emilie set the lasagna in the oven, then brought the wine glasses over while Sylvie fetched the bottle.

"I heard about your grandfather," Sylvie said, sliding onto the bench on one side and sounding as if she wasn't sure whether she should add "I'm sorry," or not.

Emilie sat across from her and reached for her glass to buy time for a response, though she needed to get some food into herself before hitting the wine too much or she'd been under this table and not very good company.

"What all did you hear?" she answered finally; carefully.

Sylvie's face told her enough.

Emilie had few memories of her father's father, and hadn't learned until his death this fall that he'd been central to the reason they'd left Montreal. She'd just been thrilled they were going to have their own farm after living in the suburbs. Before the move, the horses in their life had all been at her grandfather's stable. He trained show horses and Liv had been his star pupil — breeding Thoroughbreds had been a side project. Emilie hadn't been as single-minded as her sister, and one of the working students had taught her in her lessons. She hadn't realized her grandfather had been a monster, and Liv the target of his lechery.

"I had no idea," she said, quietly. "How did I have no idea?"

"People are good at keeping those kinds of secrets," Sylvie said. "It makes sense they were trying to protect you."

"From what? From knowing what my sister went through?"

"You were pretty young when it was happening. We were just carefree kids back then."

"I know, but wouldn't you think some time in the last twelve years someone would fill me in?"

"So who finally did?"

"Liv. She's actually getting therapy, thank goodness. She decided she needed to be the one to explain why sometimes she's been a little strange. And it's not like my parents did anything wrong. They didn't sweep it under the rug once they knew. They got the hell out of Dodge. But...I don't know. I wish I'd known so much sooner."

"Would it have changed anything?"

"Well... it just would have been nice to understand. But it's out there now, so that much is good. And in two days, wonder of wonders, she's getting married!"

Sylvie raised her glass. "To romance."

Emilie snorted, but clinked her glass to Sylvie's anyway.

"What was that for?" Sylvie asked.

"Are you seeing anyone?" Emilie deflected.

"Oh, come on. You have to tell me."

"It's silly," Emilie insisted.

"Doesn't matter. We used to be best friends."

"When we were ten." Emilie laughed, then reflected, "Other than the fact we weren't drinking wine back then, it almost feels like no time has passed at all."

While Roger Cloutier and his wife, Hélène, had relocated to

Ontario not long after the Lachances, Sylvie had stayed behind and lived with an aunt and uncle to finish secondary school, and now attended university in Montreal. They'd kept in touch since the move through letters and emails.

"So," Sylvie prompted. "Tell me."

"I think the lasagna must be warm by now." She leapt up.

"You are so bad!"

"I just need more wine to tell my story, and I have to eat something first. It's that ridiculous."

To speed things up, Sylvie helped her, cutting the layered entrée and sliding generous pieces onto the plates Emilie produced. They returned to the table.

After a few forkfuls and more wine, Sylvie was drumming her fingers on the table with a pointed look. Emilie sat up, leaning against the back of the bench.

"I'm going to meet my future husband at the wedding. Or before, I expect." *Tomorrow. It would be tomorrow.* She felt a stupid flutter in her stomach.

"Your future husband?" Sylvie's lips twisted in amusement. "Tell me more!"

"It's a joke," Emilie explained. "Nate has a younger brother. Ever since pretty well everyone learned that, they decided that he and I are destined."

"Ah. Because of your little crush on Nate?"

"It was not a crush. Not a real crush, anyway."

"Oh, I don't know about that."

"Fine, maybe it started out that way, but I was able to recognize it as that. I didn't waste time languishing over the fact that he would never be mine." She swept the back of her hand to her brow dramatically. "And, to be honest, once I got to know him a bit, I figured out he had some baggage and I wasn't into that, so I fully supported his thing for Liv. Well — except when he was seeing Faye, when I had to support that.

After telling him to be careful." She shook her head, remembering how all that turned out. "He should have listened to me!"

Sylvie laughed. "We've obviously been slacking in our correspondence these last few years, because I missed all of that."

"It's been a rollercoaster, let me tell you."

"So," Sylvie prodded again. "Let's hear about the brother. What do you know about him?"

"He's my age. He's a professional hockey player."

"Nice." Sylvie nodded approvingly. "Though how does a jockey have a brother who's a professional hockey player?"

Emilie shrugged. "Who knows."

"Do you know what he looks like?"

"I've only seen a few pictures. Faye has met him, though."

"And?"

"She says he's pretty hot."

"Sounds promising. I'll definitely need an update when you get back."

"It's ridiculous though, right?"

"Why? There's no harm in believing, right?"

"Sure." *I want to believe.* It would be nice if the final piece of the puzzle — career, obsessive hobby, relationship — could be pressed so easily into place.

Emilie cleared the table, then poured more wine. She met Sylvie's eyes, solemn as she sipped. "Do you want to talk about your mom?"

Sylvie set her glass down, pressing her fingers against the base. "I don't even know where to start to talk about that. I still can't believe it's happening. Not my mom, you know? She's the one who takes care of everyone else. It's not so easy for her to let herself be taken care of, so that makes it even harder. At least the surgery is behind her, but the chemo... it's just so..."

Sylvie trailed off, brushing light brown hair from her face that was so much like the hair her mother would by now be losing. "Do you know the survival rate for ovarian cancer is only thirty-five percent? It's terrifying."

Emilie was too practical to offer false reassurances. "When I get back — anything you need, just let me know, okay?"

Sylvie nodded, blinking back tears. "Thanks, Em. Do you need help with anything? That would actually help me, you know? Having something else to do, as a distraction."

"I'm sure I can find lots for you to help with. Both here on the farm and at Triple Shot. You in?"

"Absolutely." Sylvie pushed away the rest of her glass. "I'd better stop, or I'll be sleeping on your couch."

"That would be okay." Emilie smiled. "But I'll get you some water."

They spent the rest of the time discussing their programs at university. It was fun to talk school with someone going through the same thing; working on a graduate degree.

"At least yours has a definitive job once you're done," Sylvie said. "I have no idea where I'll work. The only thing I can think of doing next is a PhD."

"Career student."

"Exactly."

When Sylvie left, she poured herself another glass of wine, because it certainly wouldn't keep till she got back from Florida. Then her curiosity got the better of her, when she should have been packing and trying to get to bed at a reasonable hour.

Nate almost never posted anything on Facebook, but he'd shared his mother's gleeful announcement that Tim had been called up from the minors because of an injury and was in the starting lineup for Calgary's game against Tampa tonight.

Would he still make it to the wedding? When did they play next?

She liked hockey, but cheered for Montreal because it was in her blood and didn't tend to watch games unless the Canadiens were playing. It was odd to tune into one in which she had no stake, though she should probably back Calgary because Nate was a huge fan, even when Tim wasn't playing, and they were a Canadian team. It had thrilled the Millers when the Flames had drafted Tim. This was a big night.

She parked in front of the big-screen TV in the basement with her glass of wine and turned the game on. What number had Nate said he'd be wearing? It gave her a funny feeling, looking for him on TV. Like wow, she knew an NHL hockey player, by a degree of separation. In reality, her sister and soon-to-be brother-in-law were far more famous and accomplished in the sports world, but somehow playing professional hockey was more relatable than training and riding racehorses — at least in Canada, where if you didn't play or follow hockey in some way, shape, or form, people looked at you like you were an alien.

What would it be like, being a hockey wife? It couldn't be easy. He'd be on the road half the time. Summers off, though.

It was the beginning of the third period. She caught his name in the play-by-play and found him on the ice. He looked small compared to most of the players. He was fast, a good skater. He should be on that CBC program, *Battle of the Blades,* where they paired hockey players with professional figure skaters. She wondered if he was nervous, or if he was thinking it was about time, because he'd worked his whole life for this moment. Now he had to earn the chance to stay there, that was all. That couldn't be easy in such a competitive sport. He looked good to her, making snappy passes and nifty moves, his stick-handling on point. Rising to the occasion.

What she really felt was envy. Envy for that focused a career path. She'd never had it. She was the proverbial Jane of all trades, master of none. Liv had been smart enough for vet school, but she'd felt so strongly about a more direct career with Thoroughbreds to go all in. Liv had made out all right, skipping out on post-secondary education. Won big races as a jockey, and trained a Queen's Plate winner less than three months after taking out her conditioner's license. Not to mention finding Nate, the most perfect match she ever could have found, who happened to be all the things: hot, smart, and an all-round nice guy. No, her sister hadn't gone wrong with her decision.

Emilie just wanted someone to come along and tell her what to do. Give her the answer: *what's the one thing I should devote my life to, where I can be happy and significant?* And was it too much to ask for her own hot, smart, all-round nice guy?

As the period wore on, she became too bleary-eyed to follow the play, barely staying awake to see Tampa Bay win, 3-1. That was anticlimactic. She should have used the time to pack. Instead, she was up till midnight, and once she finished, she was exhausted. That wake-up call was going to hurt.

CHAPTER 7

"Wake up, Emilie. We're landing."

She was wedged against the armrest, the window seat obviously wasted on her. At least she hadn't done something even more embarrassing, like falling asleep on Dean's shoulder.

Faye and Will were across the aisle. They'd lucked out on fellow passengers agreeing to swap seats so they could at least sit in pairs, capitalizing on their story about the wedding, and overall holiday cheer — or the prospect of escaping Toronto's cold for a few days.

"Sorry I was such a bad company," she mumbled, peeling herself off the glass and rubbing crusties out of her eyes.

"That's all right," Dean said, stooping, half-crouched as he waited for space to maneuver. At his height, it must've been an uncomfortable flight. "You needed the sleep. And I needed to catch up on movies."

"I can't remember the last time I watched a movie." Maybe if she stayed awake on the way home, she could do just that.

Dean extracted her carry-on from the overhead compartment and passed it to her. Like the other three, she'd carefully packed so she didn't need to check any baggage. They were only here for two days, after all. She rested it in the seat he'd vacated while they waited for a chance to fit into the aisle.

"What's the agenda?" She turned to Faye once they were finally free from the plane and following the signs to customs.

"I worked it out on the flight. Just texting it to Liv now, though really, she has no choice but to comply."

After they cleared customs, the next stop was the car-rental desk. As long as they were in the air-conditioned terminal, Emilie could pretend it still felt like Christmas, taking in the decorations and ignoring glimpses out the windows that showed sun and blue sky and absolutely no snow. Once they were outside, she could no longer deny it was warm and humid and there were palm trees, the ocean just a stone's throw away. She left thoughts of the approaching holiday behind and switched to wedding mode. It might be normal for locals to feel festive with their determined decorations, but it all seemed so out of place to her. The cold and snow and the holiday feels would be waiting for her back in Ontario.

Now, they only had an hour and a half drive up I-95 to get to their destination. Dean got behind the wheel, and Emilie insisted Will, given he was much taller than her, ride shotgun. Faye agreed, adding that it would let her and Emilie talk about what needed to be done. Which was a brilliant plan, except Emilie fell asleep again.

"Where's the closest Starbucks?" Faye's voice finally roused her from her slumber. "We need to get this girl some coffee, or we might as well just leave her at the hotel."

Emilie grinned despite the crimp in her neck, recognizing the town of Stuart. And she knew where the closest Starbucks was. "Just ahead. Did you figure out the plan without me?"

"Yes," Faye said. "Liv and Nate are done work and already

on the beach, so once we check into the hotel, we'll head out there."

Emilie shoved down her disappointment. She wanted to go to the barn, visit with the horses, talk to Jay, and apologize for missing his race at Woodbine. Chances were she wouldn't be able to get away from the farm to come down here again when he ran.

Double shot latte in hand, Emilie set her bag on the bed at the hotel, then adjusted the air conditioning. She didn't dare sit down, because she'd probably fall asleep again despite the coffee. First order: a change of clothes. She hopped in the shower first, then decided on a sundress — over her bathing suit — and pulled towel-dried hair into a ponytail.

Dean was already at the car when she got there, but Faye and Will had yet to appear. She felt rejuvenated now, shoulders bared to the warm rays, caffeine infusion in progress as she took another sip from her cup.

"That doesn't look like beach wear, Dean," she scolded, sizing up the lightweight grey slacks and a pale yellow golf shirt he wore. He kind of blended with the silver rental car.

He shrugged. "I didn't think swimming in the ocean was part of the schedule."

"There are some things you just make time for. Did you bring shorts? You're on vacation for a few hours, can't you look like it?"

"You're a bossy one, Miss Emilie. Don't you think I get enough of that from my sister?" But there was only affection in his smile as he chided her.

She grinned. "Fine. Dress yourself, then. Just don't whine to me when you're sweltering in the sand. And by the way — have I told you how happy I am that you came?" None of them had been sure he would.

"I'd like to see Payson while we're here. I hope we can fit

60

that in," Dean said, ignoring her comment and tucking away his phone.

"You've never been?" she said. "I want to visit for sure. I hope we'll have time, too."

"Time for what?" Faye approached, looking fresh in sandals and a patterned sundress of her own, Will trailing.

"To go to Payson," Emilie said.

"Feel free to do that tomorrow morning while Will and I sleep in. Liv's insisting on going in to gallop, can you believe that?"

Emilie could. Liv was her sister, after all. The only acceptable way to start a day was on the back of a horse, so why would her wedding day be any different?

She climbed into the back seat of the car again with Faye and managed to stay awake for the drive to the coast. Last winter she'd enjoyed the luxury of staying at the condo on the beach with Liv and Cory — Emilie's friend who'd come down to gallop for the winter and was back again this year, even though she'd spent the season at Woodbine as an apprentice jockey. She was excited to see Cory, however brief their visit would be. This time, Cory was staying with the assistant trainer, Jo, in a condo in town.

Liv and Nate already had colour, as if just being down here their skin remembered last winter's tan — but how could that be, when they'd only arrived themselves last night? Maybe it was a glow of anticipation. It felt like a repeated theme in Emilie's head: she never would have thought her sister would appear that way the day before her wedding. This was not a brave show. That look was genuine. And Emilie felt it again, that tiny twist of, she had to admit — resentment.

Both of them were dressed appropriately, what clothing they wore pulled on over swimwear. Faye eyed them suspiciously before following the hugs Emilie lavished on them.

"What's it been, Em, three days?" Nate laughed at her.

"And thousands of miles," she retorted. "I'm allowed." It wasn't about the time that had passed since she'd seen them last; it was about the time that would pass when she went back home.

After releasing Nate, she glanced around nervously. Her parents weren't there yet, but she should go say hi to Connie and Reid Miller.

"You can relax," Nate said. "Tim's not here."

Part disappointment, part relief. That's what she felt. "Why not?

"He's sleeping at the hotel."

He's obviously my soulmate, then. Because as much as she was happy to be part of this, she was not done with her need to nap. "How does he get away with that and I don't?"

"Hockey pros get VIP status," Will said wryly.

"Besides, Emilie, you slept on the plane," Faye said. "You slept in the car. You should be rested."

But no, no, she was not. It was as if finally getting some sleep left her feeling more tired. *I need more, more. I need to bank hours for when I get back to my normal life.* Why didn't it work that way? She'd been running on adrenaline.

"Dean will have to be my stand-in, then." She looped her arm through his and looked up hopefully. To his credit, he merely slid his eyes to her with an unsure flick. She whispered, "Sorry!" And for a beat, she wished Dean was her wedding party partner and not some guy she didn't know — the one snoozing shamelessly in a hotel room.

She released Dean when she caught sight of her parents and flew over to greet them with a fresh flurry of hugs. It had been weeks since she'd seen them, so her exuberance was totally justified.

Faye whipped everyone into position, but if this was a

rehearsal party, it was the epitome of casual — which wasn't a surprise, because that was the theme for the whole wedding. No stuffy church exchanging of vows for her sister. Emilie was sure if Liv could've gotten permission, a horse would have been part of the ceremony. Of course, the only realistic choice would have been the stable pony, Paz, because the horses in training were theoretically too high strung. The truth of it was, Paz would have a meltdown out here, and Jay would be a much better choice. Jay — although he was a chestnut four-year-old Thoroughbred colt — was the most tractable horse Emilie knew. Except their father would have a conniption fit if they brought the best horse in his stable to the beach for a photo op. Still, it would have been fun.

"You're a good sport," she said to Dean when the run-through was over.

"Story of my life," he said dryly.

Emilie patted his arm consolingly.

"Now we're going into town for dinner," Faye announced.

"And Tim will absolutely show up for that."

Emilie hadn't noticed Nate sneak up until he fed those words into her ear. "Why?" she asked.

"Food. He's not going to miss a free meal."

Athletes required sleep and nourishment more than they needed to rehearse walking and standing around. She could respect that. He was a guy. It was unlikely he was excited about this event.

"Sit with me?" she begged Dean, clinging to him as they walked into the restaurant.

"Shouldn't you be sitting with your betrothed?" he teased.

"Not you, too?" She sighed. "Be careful, or I'll set *you* up."

"I might trust you to do that more than anyone else, Miss Emilie."

She didn't know why he called her that. Just another one of

her big brothers. He'd always think of her as the eleven-year-old she'd been when her family had first moved to Ontario.

That was the appeal of Tim. He didn't know her in the context of her circle. He didn't know her at all. She curled her toes in her sandals and tried to will away the flutter in her stomach as they gathered at the table and gave their drink orders to the server. Nate's parents hadn't arrived yet; they were swinging by the hotel to pick Tim up. "Wouldn't It Be Nice" played in her head. *You're getting ahead of yourself, Emilie.*

Nate pushed back his chair and stood, bringing her out of her reverie and tipping her off that his family had arrived. She glanced over her shoulder and spotted Connie and Reid, and a third person who must be Tim, because his features and expression almost looked copied from his father. It was as if a sculptor had started with the same mould, then smoothed out some lines; darkened the hair and added some muscle.

She couldn't tell what colour his eyes were from here — and would most certainly not let herself get foolishly lost in them over dinner in an attempt to find out. He was taller than Nate by a good four inches. Not a terrible thing at all. The open-necked dress shirt he wore fit him perfectly, from impressive shoulders down. And it was periwinkle. She had to wonder: had his mother bought it for him, or was he just a natty dresser?

Stop staring, Emilie. She dragged her eyes away before she got any further and focused on her plate instead. Then reached for her water glass and took a gulp. The saving grace was, during the introductions, only Liv, Nate and Will left their chairs to greet Tim, everyone else remaining seated. Emilie was good with informal. Tim probably wouldn't even remember her name, Nate rattling them off as he went around the table.

"I guess you met Faye at the hospital, and Liv's parents,

Claude and Anne. Dean is Faye's brother, then next to him is Emilie, Liv's sister."

Tim only met her eyes briefly as she gave him a small smile. He sat next to Nate, on the other side of the table from her, but not quite opposite, which was all right. It would have been too awkward had he been directly across from her. She squirmed in her chair, then hiccuped. *Oh no.* Reaching for her water, she sipped again. And hiccuped again. *Great.*

"Don't mind me," she said, and prayed everyone didn't start with sure-fire remedies. Nate she gave an especially hard glare. There was only one time in recent memory she'd been afflicted with hiccups, and Nate was the guy who liked to scare them out of people. He'd totally spooked her, but it hadn't solved the problem. They all eventually ignored her as the server returned to take food orders, and the hiccups disappeared on their own.

Every so often throughout the meal, she stole glances at Tim. She listened when he answered questions others asked him, but he never directly addressed her. She wasn't usually this quiet, but the discomfort of the situation was getting to her. It was only her, she'd bet. Nate probably hadn't made the same suggestion about the two of them to Tim. Not like Faye and Liv.

Off-handedly at first. Casually. It was a joke that had been repeated so many times since it had become expected. Tim just hadn't been let in on the secret yet.

Nate has a younger brother, you know. Wink, wink. Which felt like pressure. But Emilie did well under pressure.

But his brother... his brother wasn't playing out to be the easy fix everyone had anticipated. She'd thought for sure there would be an opportunity to exchange a few words with him — they were in complementary roles tomorrow, shouldn't there be some talk of that, if only to acknowledge it? But he left much the way he came; silently, slipping out after his parents. It was silly, but she felt let down.

He was probably just as tired as she was, plucked out of the usual rapid pace of his life for this. He had played in Tampa last night, after all. That was it. At the wedding, they'd have a chance to chat. She'd get to know him then.

Both Liv and Nate had nixed any talk of a Stag and Doe; there had been no bridal shower. Faye put her foot down for tonight, though.

"This is the last time all three of us will be single," she said, and banished the guys, making them take Nate away. Not that there would be a wild night for any of them. They went to the hotel, and Faye, Liv and Emilie claimed the condo.

Wine and ice cream were an unlikely combination, but it had always been their go-to for girls' night. It had been a while since they'd done it, at least like this. The last time Emilie remembered was the night before Liv ran Chique in the Breeders' Stakes, poised on the brink of a possible Canadian Triple Crown. Liv had been more nervous that evening than she was now. For the first time Emilie could remember, she would say her sister was at peace. It was a wonder to see, and she wondered more when she might find it herself.

CHAPTER 8

The fairytale came to life — even if the way here had been messy.

She wasn't sure her sister believed in a higher power, but Emilie did, because this was a miracle. A declaration before God and friends and family; a proclamation of faith in something so elusive: *till death do us part*. If Liv could find true love, anyone could. Just how was it she'd managed on her first go?

Emilie didn't know if the tears she shed were of joy, for what was happening before her, or sadness, for herself. More like self-pity. It was just so backward that Liv, who had been so opposed to the idea of a relationship, let alone marriage, was standing here in front of her, tying the proverbial knot with the guy everyone was, secretly, madly in love with.

Sure, Emilie admitted to having a crush when Nate first started working on the farm. But it hadn't taken her long to figure out he'd dragged a boatload of baggage with him when he'd made the move from Alberta to Ontario. And she was too smart to legitimately fall for a guy who needed to be fixed. Liv hadn't intended to fall at all, and needed plenty of fixing herself, so Emilie wasn't making a point about her sister's common sense. The connection between Liv and Nate had not been immediate by any stretch of the imagination. They'd worked through the brokenness to be standing here today. Emilie was so proud of both of them.

The problem for Emilie was, being little-sister-zoned was worse than being friend-zoned. Which brought her back to the intriguing prospect of the younger brother, standing behind Nate's best friend and best man, Will. Tim once again looked delectable, this time in his formal attire — though like a hunter class on a hot day, jackets were excused. A lovely breeze kept it from being sweltering on the beach.

When he glanced over, he looked away just as quickly, appearing entirely bored by the ceremony. Swept up in the romance of the day, Emilie was inspired. This would be a challenge, but she was up for it. Because that challenge shared DNA with Nate. Under the shell Tim exhibited, there had to be something good.

Why couldn't it be her turn? Why couldn't this be fate?

She waited for that dramatic line: *speak now, or forever hold your peace!* But it didn't come. Maybe they didn't do that anymore and she watched too many romantic movies. Still, she glanced over the guests, and locked in on Dean's expression. He appeared so serious, until he noticed her, and smiled. It wasn't his turn, either.

The officiant concluded the service with those time-honoured words as the freshly hitched couple grinned at each other. Both of them looked giddy. It was ridiculously cute. Her sister? Cute? Nate, sure, but it was never a description Emilie would have attached to Liv. More proof anything could happen.

The kiss, though, was way more than cute. It made Emilie

curl her toes into the sand, and she found Tim staring at her, his eyes dark, which only amplified the heat creeping up her neck. That gaze was steely. Almost like he disapproved. Of what? The wedding, or her?

Faye whooped loudly in her ear, breaking their eye-lock. Then Liv grabbed Nate's hand and dragged him toward the surf, the look on Nate's face suggesting it wasn't part of the script. After a couple of steps, he started running with her, splashing into the water. They surfaced, kissing again before emerging with apparent reluctance from the waves. Good thing the undertow hadn't swept them away because they hadn't signed anything yet. Not that this was about a piece of paper.

Hanging onto each other, laughing and dripping, Emilie saw with an undeniable clarity that her sister was, most definitely, in love with Nate Miller, like she'd given herself to it, just as the words they'd recited demanded. For a long time Emilie had known Liv loved him, even if Liv had difficulty admitting it — and certainly vocalizing it — but there was a subtle difference, wasn't there? Loving someone was a steady, enduring thing. Being in love was whimsical, and possibly transient. They'd all given Liv a hard time on various levels about her reluctance, but in hindsight, Emilie felt she'd done it right. Foundation first, fun later. Who ever would have thought her sister would give her a model to which she'd aspire?

When they disappeared inside, the guests milling about hesitantly, Faye stage-whispered, "Do you think they'll come back?"

"That will be very interesting to see," Emilie admitted, grinning. "I say we check on the status of the champagne, and if they're not back in twenty, we go ahead without them."

Faye laughed, then looped her arm through Emilie's. "Brilliant plan." Then she leaned in, whispering again. "Have you talked to Tim yet?"

"No." Emilie frowned. "He's only glared at me so far."

"He's just shy."

"If you say so."

"I met him at the hospital the day of Nate's surgery. He and the father didn't talk much, but Connie's lovely. We'll go chat with her, then when the dancing starts you can make your move." She elbowed Emilie gently, flashing one of her wicked smiles.

"I don't like my chances. Where's that champagne?"

They busied themselves by furnishing everyone with a glass. Then Nate and Liv reappeared, mostly dry.

"So much for the hair." Faye sighed, taking in the state of Liv's damp tresses, and handed them both a flute of pale, bubbly liquid before taking one of the two Emilie held. "That was quite the impromptu performance."

"Sorry." Liv smiled, brushing a damp strand from her face and tucking it behind her ear. "It felt right."

"Someone should make a toast," Faye said, glancing around to be sure everyone had a glass. "Get over here, Will. Isn't that your job?"

Will made his way to Faye's side, draping an arm over her shoulders. "I thought we said no speeches."

Tim lagged, avoiding their core group to stand with his parents instead. *Fine,* Emilie thought, then smirked when she caught Nate watching her watching Tim, an eyebrow quirked at her and a smile playing on his lips.

"I don't care," Emilie hissed, then held her glass out, projecting, "To my sister and brand new brother-in-law, and things that will last forever."

Faye nodded. "Cheers! Well done, you two."

Echoed words and the chime of clinking crystal bounced

through the small gathering. Emilie couldn't stop watching Liv and Nate. The way they kept looking at each other was so beautiful. And it was better than chancing another glance at Tim.

There was no band. Not even a fancy stereo system — which was kind of funny, given both Nate and Will were complete sound snobs. It was casual, casual, casual — probably so as not to tick off the neighbours as much as for Liv's comfort level, seeing as this was a private beach. Will and Nate put together the music, and the dancing began, playing from an iPhone through a wireless speaker. Once Liv and Nate started, the rest of them had to do their part. Which meant, whether they liked it or not, Tim and Emilie were paired up for the first dance. Crunch time.

She was very aware of him. She'd never been this close to a professional hockey player before, and hadn't expected him to be this big, somehow. On television he'd been just a tiny speck on the screen, and visibly smaller than most of his teammates. And he was way bigger than Nate. Like Nate on steroids. Yes, she did compare everyone to Nate, it seemed. And not that she thought Tim was actually on steroids. But who knew?

Though taller than Nate, Tim didn't have the same height as Will or Dean. It was all about muscle mass. Emilie had to stop herself from squeezing the bicep under her hand to test if it really was as rock-hard as it seemed under her touch — the one she kept as light as she possibly could. Her heart could stop thumping in her chest any time now. She didn't dare look up at him. Her knees felt as if they were going to give out, just because of his nearness, and the suggestion she'd been hearing for a year now. No guy had ever disrupted her respiration like this. Nope, not even Nate.

She tried to come up with clever things to say. It normally wasn't a problem for her, but in this moment, with all the build-up, she was struck dumb. If she tried to talk about hockey, or mentioned she'd seen him play the other night, she'd sound like a groupie. What was the hockey equivalent of paddock girl or jockey jumper?

"I bet the temperature sure beats Calgary right now," she tried. *Great, Emilie. Talk about the weather.* But she was desperate, and it was a safe topic for conversation. It said, *I don't care if my circle of friends has decided we are fated to be together and you seem to have missed the memo.* "It was nice to get out of Ontario, though I wouldn't want to spend Christmas here."

He looked down at her. His eyes were brown, not blue like Nate's, the breeze lifting his tawny hair away from them. "I guess."

Even when every muscle in his body was protesting this tradition, he had a grace about him. Athletes, right? Nate was a great dancer. Connie Miller had done competitive ballroom in her younger days and must've taught Tim, too. That's probably why he was such a good skater. So either he didn't like dancing, or he just didn't like dancing with her.

"How long of a flight was it for you?" Then she felt like an idiot, remembering he hadn't flown from Calgary with his parents.

He shrugged. "I only had to come from Tampa. I rented a car and drove."

"How long did that take?"

"About three hours."

"It was just over three hours to fly from Toronto. But once you add in the airport time, you probably came out ahead." He hadn't asked, and looked like he didn't care. Okay, we've covered the weather, and travel. Um... what next? "This is a great song. It's so perfect for their first dance."

When he raised one eyebrow, he looked a lot like Nate, just shrouded. "I don't even know who this is."

"You don't know Poe? What kind of stuff do you listen to?" Nate had great taste in music, though this song was totally for Liv. It was "Amazed." It was beautiful and haunting and spoke so much of her sister's journey with him. *You change the equation I add up to.* No one had needed to tell Nate who Poe was. If Tim had bad taste in music, it could be a deal-breaker. But Tim didn't deign her worthy of a response.

Now she really wished she were dancing with Nate. They wouldn't be talking, because they'd be enjoying themselves too much. She glanced past Tim's shoulder to find the fun brother, presently coercing her sister into doing more than shuffling her feet in the sand. Liv was laughing and doing a pretty good job. Emilie threw a grin up at Tim.

He scowled, eyes going from bored to steely again, stopping her joy in an instant. "Listen," he said, his voice flat. "I don't know what my brother told you, but if he said he was going to set us up, I'm not interested, okay? I'm only even here because my mom said I had to come."

"What are you, fifteen? I'm not after you, okay?" Emilie snapped. It helped cover her embarrassment, like he'd found her out. "And I'm here because I want to be, so I really rather not waste my time with someone who can't take a joke." She gave him a fake smile and stomped off. *More champagne, stat!*

The iPhone launched into the next tune. Emilie didn't care. What came after the first dance, anyway? Did it matter? She didn't think Liv and Nate were too hung up on decorum this afternoon.

"Obviously that went well." Faye appeared at her elbow.

"Fabulously. He wasn't so shy that he held back telling me he wants nothing to do with me. As if I even asked. What was that? And how can *that* be related to Nate?"

"I'm going to be the one to remind you that you have a very rose-coloured-glasses view of Nate."

Emilie snorted. "So you're saying...?"

"Nate isn't that perfect, either. Maybe you're getting to see the bad side of the brother up front, and you've yet to discover the good side."

"First impressions, Faye. First impressions."

"C'mon. We get to dance for fun now."

"Cory!" Emilie called, waving her friend over from the sidelines to join them. This would be their chance to catch up, and her chance to forget about Tim. The tempo of the music picked up, and three of them bounced in the sand, arms flailing and hair flinging, laughing and breathless.

A few upbeat songs, then they convinced Connie to give them mini ballroom lessons. Will set up the music, and Connie paired with Faye. Nate held out his hand to Emilie and bowed. Emilie curtsied in return and grasped his fingers. Liv laughed from the fringes of the sandy dance floor with the three guys who looked just as glad as she was to be watching, not taking part: Dean, Will, and Mr. Grumpypants.

Emilie dug out her most charming smile, directing it at her new brother-in-law, and wiped her sweaty brow with the back of her hand before resting it on his arm. "I don't care what Faye says, you're all right, Nate."

He laughed. "Oh, great. What part of the past is Faye dredging up this afternoon? And why?"

She decided answering that would require revealing too much, so she pretended to trip over his feet instead. "Oh — crap! Sorry! How did that step go?"

Nate smirked at her, like he'd figured out she was avoiding something; he just didn't know what. He let her off the hook. This wasn't the time to get into it. But she kind of wished they could.

CHAPTER 9

It was a beautiful evening, and the pool was completely deserted when they returned to the hotel, leaving Liv and Nate to themselves at the condo on the beach. Emilie was tired, but she was going for a dip. She fished her suit from her bag, slipped out of her bridesmaid dress, and put the bikini on. With a t-shirt for a coverup, she tamed her wind and dance-blown hair back with an elastic, grabbed a towel from the bathroom, and prayed no one else had the same idea.

Someone did, but she decided not to let that stop her. She unlatched the gate, clicking it shut as quietly as she could behind her — as if that would disturb anything. When she turned toward the pool, lit from under the surface so it sparkled enticingly, she stopped dead.

The someone was Tim, legs stretched in front of him on a lounge chair at the opposite end. If he'd seen her, he was ignoring her now, staring at his phone.

Whatever. He wasn't going to ruin this for her. Even if he was shirtless. *Ahem.* Muscles. Pecs, and abs, and deltoids and quads. Which weren't a surprise, because she'd already figured out he was stunningly fit, as he'd have to be to play hockey at the level he did. But exposed in all their albeit-pale glory under his brooding frown like a shirtless viking man... *oh my*. She gulped. He was actually better-looking than Nate.

She didn't need to like him to appreciate the view. Such a shame; or maybe it was the broodiness that made him so attractive. Did he ever smile? Maybe that face fell apart when he did, its unblemished surface cracking because it wasn't pliable. Because smiling seemed to be a rare thing, so she'd bet that skin was brittle.

She was making a fool of herself. *Stop staring, Emilie.* She tossed her towel on a chair, peeled her t-shirt off — take that bare-chested hockey man — and stepped to the edge.

The water was barely below bathtub temperature. She supposed they kept it there for the retirees who came down here to escape the cold back home. It wasn't exactly conducive to swimming for exercise — better for floating — but she'd do a few laps through its short length.

She loved the feel of the water slipping around her, even though it wasn't particularly refreshing. Counting the strokes from one end to the other so subsequently she could close her eyes and just swim, she told herself to stop wondering if he was watching her. She wasn't entirely successful, but decided her reaction to his aloofness wasn't about him rejecting her, not really. It was about her. She must be doing something to repel the right kind of guy. Time for the friend- and sister-zoning to end. It wasn't going to be with Tim Miller. That was obvious. And that was fine.

She declared herself open to Mr. Right-for-her. He wasn't here, but he was out there. Somewhere.

Stopping in the shallow end, she threw her head back and gazed upward. Too much light pollution to see anything; to tell if it was cloudy or clear. No north star to locate and direct her.

That was fine. Her phone had a compass. As did the pilot of the plane that would take her back to Ontario tomorrow afternoon. She floated over to the steps, and climbed out, then retrieved her towel.

As she dried off, she faced him, unabashed. Should she give him another chance? If Faye was right and he was shy, maybe he'd be nicer with no one around. She would just be friendly. Because she was over the fantasy.

He preempted the possibility. Got up, strode down the long side of the deck to the little gate. Didn't even say goodnight.

Just in case she'd had any remaining illusions. They faded like so many wisps trailing in the air he pushed aside. Got it. She stuck her tongue out at his back for good measure and pulled the t-shirt over her head. He might have that whole Viking god thing going on, but right now all he looked like was a beautiful letdown.

After she rinsed off in the shower in her room, she pulled on baggy shorts and a dry shirt, grabbed her room key, stuffed a twenty in her pocket, then went to the little convenience store at the gas station to buy a big bottle of water and some chocolate. Three different bars. American chocolate bars sucked for the most part, but this was an emergency. Before reaching the checkout, she added a bag of white cheese popcorn; some salty to balance the sweet.

She skipped up the stairs at the end of the block of rooms and ran into Dean coming out of his. He raised his eyebrows at her bag of snacks.

"Where are you going?" she asked.

He held up a plastic bucket. "Ice."

"You have alcohol?"

"Yes."

"I'll share my snacks if you share your booze."

Dean laughed. "Sure. But don't forget we have to be up early tomorrow to leave for the airport."

"I'm not suggesting we get drunk." Just a short pity party for both of them. Then it was time to move on.

Famous last words.

Dean wasn't messing around. Maybe she'd misjudged how hard this was hitting him. He had a bottle of vodka, and a bottle of fresh-squeezed orange juice, and poured generous quantities from each over ice. Emilie accepted the plastic cup he handed her. The apprehension on her face must've been obvious.

"You pour a mean screwdriver, Mr. Taylor."

"We're in the land of cheap alcohol, Miss Emilie. It's our responsibility as Canadians to imbibe."

And so she did.

She was not going to talk about whatever sympathy she might have for Dean's plight. She would not lament her own lack of a love life; her failure to land the big fish. There were other things to talk about.

"This might be the best screwdriver I've ever had," she announced.

"It's the fresh-squeezed orange juice," he said. "Nice, isn't it?"

"It is," she agreed, though the one-to-one ratio was already threatening to numb her fingers. She shoved a handful of popcorn in her mouth, then held the bag out to him. "So what should I do? Am I in denial, planning to be a physiotherapist? Am I going to regret it? I should finish school, right?"

Dean had abandoned a master's program to take over his father's training business after his parents died. While it might have seemed valiant on the surface, Dean readily admitted conditioning racehorses was what he'd always wanted to do.

"I can't tell you, Emilie. You'll have to figure that out on your own."

"Do you ever wish you'd stayed? Finished grad school? Been... what would you have been, anyway? I should probably know that already. Some friend, eh?"

"You mean, so I'd have something to fall back on?" He chuckled, the chair seeming too small for his sprawled form. "No. Not even when things have been bad. I feel guilty that my parents' death gave me my out. But you don't hate what you're doing like I did. You like people, Emilie. You want to help them as much as the animals. That's why you're so good at this aftercare stuff. You get both sides."

She'd never thought about it that way. She'd ponder it more... when her head was a little clearer. It didn't take much vodka for her to feel very drunk, very fast. Even waiting for the ice to melt and dilute it didn't help. Neither did trying to alternate swallows of alcohol with popcorn and water.

"It was a lovely wedding, even if we were both spurned in our own way." She grinned, unable to avoid the topic she'd just told herself she wasn't going to broach. She was blaming the vodka. "We're the nice ones, Dean. Why are we both still single?"

"Can't fight with destiny, right?"

"Destined to be single?" she said, then sighed dramatically. "It's okay Tim doesn't like me. It's not his fault everyone else shoved the idea on us."

"He's just afraid of you. You're a force to be reckoned with, Miss Emilie."

Her nose burned as she snorted, almost sputtering out her most recent sip of vodka and orange. "Don't say that. That's so cliché. And also, I'm doomed, if it's true."

"Why are you doomed?"

"Because if that's why guys don't like me — because I'm too self-sufficient — what hope do I have?"

"Not all men will be scared off by that."

"Most men aren't as evolved as you, Dean."

It was his turn to snort. "I'm evolved? I think somehow you've confused that with resigned. Or just trained. After living with my sister all these years."

"I think you're actually very old-fashioned, in a way. You want all that, but it has to be right. And as much as I understand your attraction to my sister, and Faye would have loved it, the two of you are too much alike. You're both too introverted and cerebral. It never would have worked."

"Thanks for that, Miss Emilie."

"Don't judge me for the truth! Liv has a sister though, you know." She laughed, having been the victim of those words. "And, she'd be much better suited to you."

Where was this going? *Too much Vodka, Emilie.* But... Dean was handsome and smart and sane... and... she calculated quickly in her head — twelve years older than her. Which might have been a big age difference when she was eleven, but now that she was twenty-three? It was nothing.

"Don't look at me like that, Emilie," he said quietly.

"Why not?" She didn't bother trying to deny it, but his laugh said there were oh, so many reasons. "Fine."

She grappled for her phone and tried to focus on the time. "I guess I should go. I'm tired of feeling sorry for myself." But when she stood, her head swam. She braced herself against the table. "I'm too drunk to walk. I'll get pulled over and lose my walking license just going to my room."

He caught her when she bobbled and scooped her up, and she could feel his laugh before he placed her on the bed.

"G'night," she mumbled, and passed out.

When she cracked her eyes open, the room was dark, save

for the glow at the edges of the curtains. Dean was still wedged in that chair, chin to his chest, and she felt terrible, subjecting him to that. And it was time to get going — late enough they'd better hurry — so it wasn't even if she could relinquish the bed to him. She rolled off it, guzzled what was left of her water, and nudged him gently.

"Dean," she whispered. "We have to get going or we're going to be late." He stirred, and she gave him a sheepish grin. "Sorry about last night."

She sneaked out the door, closing it as quietly as she could as she glanced first to the left, then to the right. Not that she had any reason to be furtive, even if it felt very much like she was doing the walk of shame with her rumpled hair, smeared makeup she hadn't bothered to remove before swimming, and throbbing temples.

The coast was clear, and her room was only two doors down. But of course, at that instant, Faye appeared from the one between hers and Dean's.

Faye's jaw dropped, eyebrows furrowing. "Did you spend the night in my brother's room?"

She should have said, "It's not what you think." But instead she averted her eyes as she brushed past Faye and mumbled, "Not now, Faye. I need a shower and I'm already late."

CHAPTER 10

Her head was out of sorts. It felt like Monday, but she knew it wasn't. The mid-week wedding was to blame. Racetrackers didn't have the same concept of a weekend that the rest of the world did. So what was today again? Wait — it was the weekend. It was Saturday. She hacked Reba on Saturdays. She'd booked the day off at the clinic. This might be her last chance for a breather before Christmas, so she was taking it. But sleeping in didn't mean ten AM or anything as indulgent as that. She was still helping Faye at the café.

Faye, who wasn't talking to her.

She'd clear that up this morning. What a scandal it would have been if Faye's suppositions were true. Was it wrong she'd enjoyed that feeling? They all expected her to always be good. And she was good — all she'd done was drink a few too many vodka and oranges, and almost-but-not-quite propositioned Dean Taylor. She drowsed an extra hour, then crawled from her bed to the shower.

Faye didn't look much brighter than she did, already up to

her elbows in work. Thank goodness for good coffee. Those eyebrows were still perfect, though, arched toward her hairline, her expression full of accusation.

"Nothing happened, okay?" She wished she could have dragged it out longer, let Faye roil in her speculation.

"But you let me think something did."

"For less than a day. I bet you didn't interrogate your brother." Though Dean had slept on the plane this time, and Faye and Will hadn't been just across the aisle. Dean has also been tight-lipped on the drive home from the airport, and though that was just how he was sometimes, it fed Emilie's deception well. "And what if I had? Why would it be wrong? You would have been fine with Liv getting together with him. Why not me?"

"All right. You've got me. I'm sorry."

"Dean will only ever see me as that eleven-year-old he first met. But your brother is a catch. I'm not sure he actually wants a girlfriend. He was just in love with an idea, with Liv." *Like me, with Tim.* Reality had come up so much shorter. "Why does everyone think there's something wrong with you if you're alone? There's nothing wrong with wanting to be alone."

"Sounds like you're trying to talk yourself into something, Em."

Or out of something. The thing was, she was fine with being alone. She didn't need a man. But was it so wrong she wanted one? "I'm waiting to hear from the Crawfords about Theo. He'll be my guy, all hairy and golden, and I shall devote my life to him. The rest of them can go stuff themselves."

Emilie split her time between helping in the kitchen and serving a steady stream of customers; some coming for coffee and a treat, or a light breakfast, others picking up packaged assortments of baked goods.

"I can't believe how many orders you're getting for cookie and treat trays," Emilie said, assembling yet another collection.

"No one wants to bake anymore. And why settle for the grocery store stuff when you can have this for a bit more?"

"You don't have to convince me. But I am starting to worry if I'm going to hate baking after this."

Faye laughed. "If that were possible, you'd get sick of horses too."

"And that'll never happen."

"I rest my case."

"You're going to have to expand to online sales."

"This is quite enough work right now, Em. But we can talk about that after the holidays."

The door jangled, someone new coming in, and Emilie ducked out to take her place behind the cash register.

"Sylvie!" She grinned.

"I had to stop by and see the famous café. I'll also have to take a box of treats or my father will never forgive me. He's been raving about them. Says they've been spoiled at the track."

"They have. Nate's even accused us of giving him a weight problem." A jockey with a pastry chef best friend was a dangerous thing. "What would you like? Straight butter tarts? We're in the middle of a Christmas cookie baking frenzy. I could set you up."

"How about half a dozen tarts today, and I'll order some cookies? My mom won't be baking this year, and this way if I don't manage any either, we'll have something."

"How's she doing?" Emilie asked cautiously. It felt like it had been weeks instead of days since she and Sylvie had talked, though Sylvie had stopped by the farm as promised in Emilie's absence and updated her with an *All is well. The place is still standing. Relax and enjoy yourself* text. She pulled a package of six butter tarts from the display cabinet. "You want a coffee? Cappuccino?"

Sylvie nodded. "That sounds like just the thing, thanks."

Faye poked her head out as Emilie fired up the espresso machine. "Faye, have you ever met Sylvie? Roger and Hélène's daughter."

Faye's face lit up, half with interest, half with concern. "I'm not sure if we have or not," she said, coming up to the counter and offering her hand. "How's your mom?"

Emilie studied Sylvie carefully when the answer still wasn't forthcoming, a sick feeling overtaking her stomach.

"She's just having a rough few days. I'm sure it'll pass."

But the worry and fear that it might not tortured her words and expression. Emilie turned off the steamer and left the carafe on the counter, coming around. Her arms encircled Sylvie and the words got caught in her throat. "I'm so sorry."

Sylvie brushed away a tear as Emilie released her.

Faye appeared at Emilie's elbow. She'd finished steaming the milk and put the drink together. "Why don't you two sit for a few minutes?" she suggested, leading the way to a table and setting the cup on the surface. "You want a cappuccino too, Em?

I've only had one. It's not too soon for a second, is it? "Thanks, Faye. I'd appreciate that."

"So what happens next?" Emilie asked, her eyes on Sylvie's face, though Sylvie was locked on the mug between her hands.

"This is just the first round of chemo. Of three, I guess. Happy New Year, eh?"

Emilie was still at a loss for words. It was heartbreaking. Hélène was only in her early fifties. It seemed far too young to be dealing with something so life-threatening.

"How's your dad holding up?"

"Oh," Sylvie sniffled, rubbing the heel of her hand to an

eye. "It's hard to know, really. He's been so absorbed in helping her. It's almost like I feel like I have to take care of him so he can take care of her."

"It's good you're here. And how are you?"

Sylvie didn't meet her eyes, her lower lip pinned between her teeth. "I feel bad I have to leave the house sometimes, but I can't fall apart in front of my mother, can I? Who do you turn to when you can't turn to your mom?"

"Us, Sylvie," Emilie said, her own voice quavering. And suddenly her own complaints about life were completely selfish and trivial.

"I think I'll be withdrawing from school for next semester. It's more important for me to stay. I'm going to need those distractions I talked about," Sylvie added, trying to smile through her tears.

"I have just the thing." Emilie did her best to smile back.

THE BEST THING about winter in Ontario? Snow hacks. Emilie handed Sylvie a shank, sizing her outfit up.

"You look as if you're dressed warm enough."

"Layers, right? These winter breeches were in my mom's closet. Go figure. Long johns under them because they didn't seem quite enough."

"Yeah, just sitting there can get chilly. You'd be fine without them if we were doing something more." She wore three layers of her own: a base layer under jeans topped with chaps, and a puffy coat. "I've got a spare helmet you can borrow. You can get on Reba, because believe it or not, even though she's just two, she's the safest thing on the farm. You'd think Twizzle would be, because he's like, twenty-five or something now, but no."

"Twizzle — I remember that name. That's Liv's old event horse, right?"

Emilie grinned. "Yeah. Now he mostly bosses around the weanling boys. I can't remember the last time anyone was on him, so this could be interesting. I've got my phone in case of emergency!" She patted her pocket. "When's the last time you rode?"

"Oh," Sylvie hesitated. "That's a very good question. High school?"

"That's not too bad. Reba will take care of you."

She let Sylvie have the old close contact saddle that collected dust between the cleanings Emilie gave it to make sure it didn't dry out. Sylvie had enough experience she'd be fine with that, and though it was pretty flat compared to a lot of the newer saddles these days, it was definitely more than the exercise saddle Emilie usually rode the filly with. She checked the fit to be sure it was passable and Reba didn't complain.

Twizzle looked like she'd dressed him up for Halloween with the exercise saddle because, while he wasn't a big horse, he was a good doer, with the rounded barrel and generous topline to prove it. He was fuzzy enough Emilie didn't think he needed a quarter sheet. She put a track bridle with rings on him. The martingale might come in handy, if only for psychological purposes. They led the horses to a mounting block outside, and Emilie made sure Sylvie was up first before getting on Twizzle, who claimed to have forgotten everything he'd ever known about standing until his rider was safely in the tack.

"Austin!" she called, hindsight nattering in her ear that she should have called him out while they were mounting for just such a situation. Oh well. She was on now. He appeared in the doorway. "Can you take our picture, please?"

He grinned, and they posed, and he promised to text it to her as they rode off.

The horses' unshod hooves crunched on the snow, Emilie leading the way, picking the path chewed up by tire tracks where the footing was secure. She hoped they got more snow. Lots and lots of it. If Sylvie was going to be around for a while to ride with, they'd have fun. It would be good for all of them; horses and humans alike.

Twizzle seemed to think galloping tack meant they should head for the track. He'd retired from racing before the move to Ontario, so she wasn't even sure he knew where the training oval was. She couldn't remember if Liv had conditioned him out there when she'd been competing with him. She did recall off the track he'd had a mouth of iron, and had probably taught Liv more about holding a tough horse than the actual horses in training. With the likes of Liv and Nicole, and even Nate and Cory, galloping the track horses now, transitioning them to new careers when they retired from racing was a breeze compared to the early days.

It was peaceful in the woods, and both women fell to silence as they traversed the narrow path, single-file. Twizzle was eager, stepping out with ears up, looking for things to spook at. Each bird that fluttered, every rabbit that scurried, set him on edge. Good thing he had a gelding-spook. He'd just drop six inches, stopping in place, and send out a snort that echoed through the trees. He wasn't a kicker, either, thankfully, because more than once Reba and Sylvie were caught off guard when the old man put on the brakes abruptly, Reba running up his well-rounded behind.

Emilie giggled, glancing back. "Sorry! You okay?"

"I'm fine. She's fine — just embarrassed." Reba backed a couple of steps as if to demonstrate her horror having bumped into her companion.

"Twizzle's the one who should be embarrassed. And he definitely does not think he's fine!" She scrubbed his neck, and he sighed, though still not convinced they weren't about to be eaten by bears out here.

The snow was deeper through the trees, and because she hadn't ridden through here since the last snowfall, they laid down a fresh track. All the evergreens were dressed in white on the topside of their branches, and it fell soundlessly to the ground when the horses brushed through. There was the stump from the perfect little tree Nate had cut only a week ago. Just a little tree. Just for her.

She wasn't sure if they were better off once they were in the clearing by the stallion barns, Twizzle's loud exhale leaving a puff of vapour in the air and punctuating his presence to the two stallions turned out in the individual paddocks in front of them. Reba strode along brightly, tiny ears up; alert, but relaxed.

"This girl's adorable," Sylvie said, and the broad smile on her face made Emilie happy.

"I love her," Emilie said. "No one thinks she'll be much of a racehorse, but I'd be quite happy to keep her."

"Would you?"

"I guess if it really comes to that, I'd have to see. I just have so much fun with her. She's the best mental health break."

"I agree. One hundred percent!" Sylvie reached down to run a hand down Reba's wooly red neck, then slid Emilie a sly grin. "So... what happened with your intended?"

Emilie rolled her eyes and waved a hand airily. Twizzle ducked away from the motion, scooting sideways. She quickly returned the hand to the reins. "Suffice to say, it was a non-event."

"Well, that's disappointing. I was looking forward to a great love-at-first-sight story."

"So was I!" Emilie said. "It wasn't meant to be."

"There are many more frogs in the pond," Sylvie said with mock wisdom.

"That's what I'm afraid of," Emilie replied, and the two of them laughed so hard it upset Twizzle, again, just when he'd started to settle down — which only made Emilie laugh more. She worked to compose herself. "The wedding was perfect, though. Faye said she was going to collect everyone's photos and post them on Facebook, so we'll check when we're back at the barn." She'd keep the story about Dean for another time. There needed to be wine for that one.

Sylvie felt comfortable enough to pull out her phone and take some photos: the requisite shots of horse ears from the saddle, and a selfie, and one of Emilie, hands full of Twizzle. It was good to see her look relaxed, her tension on hold for a little while.

"What about you, Sylvie? Any prospects in Montreal?"

Sylvie shook her head. "None. I'm married to my lab, anyway."

It took Emilie a split-second to realize she meant laboratory, not Labrador. A smile came to her face as she thought of Norma's little nuggets of coal, and she wondered if she could go visit again, even though she wasn't getting a puppy. Hopefully there would be an email from Theo's breeder waiting for her at the end of their ride.

Twizzle kept his wits about him, just barely, the rest of the way back to the barn. If he hadn't been such a basket case, Emilie would have suggested a little canter on the track if Sylvie had been up for it. Reba didn't take a hold; she would have been fine. Maybe next time.

They dismounted outside and Emilie loosened the girth a hole and ran up her stirrups, waiting while Sylvie did the same. She let Sylvie go into the barn first.

"Good ride?" Austin rolled the feed cart down the aisle, wheels squeaking.

Twizzle side-stepped, snorting through flared nostrils. "You're such a goofball," Emilie said to the old gelding. "I should have galloped you for a couple of miles instead."

"It was wonderful," gushed Sylvie. "Why is it you go years without riding, then when you get on again you wonder what could ever have taken you away?"

"What do you want us to do with them, Austin? Back out? Stay in?" Emilie asked.

"They can stay in. Looks like we'll be finished soon, so I thought it would be nice to let the gang get out of here early."

Emilie nodded, and they led the horses to their stalls. She'd been wrong about Austin. He'd proved himself reliable, after all. The farm was in good order, the horses happy. Spending the afternoon with Sylvie made her reevaluate her Christmas plans; things would be fine here, and her mom was right. She should make an effort to get to know her grandmother. And even if it was strange and awkward, it felt more important than ever to be with her parents this year.

Once they'd put away the tack and brushed the horses and picked their feet, Emilie uncovered her phone and found Faye had tagged her in numerous photos.

"I don't know where Faye found the time to do this," she said, Sylvie leaning into her shoulder as she flipped through the images.

"They're all great," Sylvie said, then whispered, "Now, show me Tim."

There were photos of him, of course. The one of him standing next to Will during the ceremony was too far away to do him justice. She took a brief tangent to put context to an image of a drenched Liv and Nate coming out of the water, then paused at one of the two of them, dried off and dancing

— *Amazed* — before continuing to flip. Then there they were, her and Tim.

She couldn't have swiped past it if she'd tried. The photo confused her. She was looking up at him, animated — she must've been talking, and the bubble had yet to be burst. He didn't look as contrary as she'd remembered; or a filter, or the afternoon sun, or something made him appear a little less like he hated her. Like whoever had taken the photo had somehow caught the one instant he wasn't scowling at her. It sucked her in, made her examine minute details of his expression in her search for clues. *Don't even bother, Emilie.*

"Is that him?"

Sylvie's question jarred her out of her introspection. "Yeah," she said, falsely chipper. "Regardless of what happened, he's totally hot, no?"

"The two of you would have made a cute couple."

"Only on the surface." She'd thought Tim would be just a subtly different version of Nate, someone with whom she could form the kind of bond Nate had with her sister, but beyond the external resemblance, he was a complete stranger. And not a very nice one.

She and Sylvie sauntered together to the end of the barn and embraced.

"Thank you so much, Em. You were right. That was just what I needed."

"Let's do it again soon. And let me know when your mom is ready for visitors, okay?"

Sylvie smiled, her face a twist of emotions before she turned and shuffled carefully over the icy surface to her car, turning to wave before she got in.

"We should probably throw some sand out there, Austin," Emilie called as she walked back toward the tack room, her eyes trying to readjust to the dark interior. "It's melted just enough this afternoon to be slippery now that the temp's dropping again."

He was distributing grain to the last few stalls. "Good idea. I'll do that before we bring in. You staying to help?"

"I can," she said. "Tell me where the sand is and I can get started on the parking area, at least."

"It's in the feed room. There's a bucket there. I can run the big one on the back of the pickup over the driveways if you think I should."

"Great. Thanks, Austin. And thanks for taking care of everything while I was gone."

"It's my job." He shrugged with an off-handed smile. "Do I get to see the wedding photos too?"

She hesitated, but only because she was recalibrating her attitude toward him. She'd had no justifiable reason not to trust that he could handle things when she was away. He hadn't let her down.

"Sure," she said, finding them again. This time she skipped quickly over the one of her and Tim with only a brief comment he was Nate's brother.

"Seems like it was a lot of fun. You looked really pretty, Emilie." He paused, the feed scoop clutched in his hands. "I was wondering—"

The way he said it, she knew what was coming. The thing was, it didn't put her on edge. *Huh.*

"Maybe we could go out for that dinner tonight?"

A few days ago, she would have brushed it off again, but after getting the brush-off herself in Florida, she was seeing things differently. It was just dinner. She'd see how it went. Who knew? There was no harm in giving it a chance.

"Sure. We can figure out what time after we're done. How's that?"

A huge grin spread over his face. "Great."

He picked her up at 5:30 in his — what was that? A Hyundai. She searched for the model name. Veloster? She'd never heard of it. It was cute. Newish. Actually looked and smelled clean, whereas her Civic was a portable tack room, or possibly even stall, with the amount of hay chaff, straw and shavings she tracked into it. Was she just a car slob? Or was he just that guy who kept his car pristine? It was definitely a guy thing.

Austin cleaned up all right. She'd been surprised when he said he wanted to take her to the restaurant in town. It was kind of a fancy place. The associated pub was a popular local hangout — one to which she and Faye, and sometimes Liv, went often. The suggestion at first brought back her resistance — everyone would hear about it, her going out with the farm manager. Was this such a good idea? Then again, why not? Let them think what they wanted to think. She could take it. And maybe something good would come out of being open to the unexpected when the whole setup with Tim had been such a major fail.

He surprised her by being able to talk about things other than horses. Not that it mattered to her — she could talk horses all night and have the time of her life. But it was intriguing. Was he just trying to impress her? Had he asked around about her to know that she cared about the topics that surfaced, like what was going on with the environment? That she'd almost gone into the field? Except that it was a hard field to define sometimes. Like it was too broad to narrow down to something she could build a career around. Too big to feel as if she could have any real impact. Too remote. That was why she'd turned to physiotherapy. Literally hands-on helping people, while expanding her own interest in physiology... which, inevitably, she translated to horses.

They came back to horses, anyway. She didn't need much

of an invitation to talk about them, and especially Thoroughbred aftercare. Turned out Austin was a good listener. Turned out he wasn't bad company.

He drove them back to the farm, stereo playing low as they continued to chat. His taste in music was acceptable, if not interesting. She'd let herself be swept away by the anticipation of Tim, then his wildly good looks, when in hindsight, it was the most ludicrous idea on the planet. Even if they had hit it off, instead of repelling each other, when would she ever see him? Austin, in contrast, was literally in her backyard.

He pulled up in front of the big empty house, putting the car in park. She could even forgive him for not driving a standard. But her parting words were sucked from her throat when he rested a hand on the edge of her seat and leaned toward her. Her eyes popped wide as she backed away, grappling for the door handle and leaping out.

Forcing a full-teeth smile to her face, she ducked down enough to meet his disgruntled expression. Why did he ruin a nice evening by doing that?

What did you really expect, Emilie?

"Thanks for dinner, Austin! See you in the morning!" Her voice was unnaturally high-pitched. She swung the door shut and he was driving away almost before it closed.

The air was crisp and the moon was bright, and she stared upward, trying to identify stars in the shadow of its brilliance. Had she overreacted? She could have endured a kiss before skipping out. It wasn't as if she'd never kissed a guy on the first date. But why, when it wasn't what she wanted? She didn't want to play along. She didn't want to pretend.

This was all Tim's fault. If he hadn't snubbed her, she never would have agreed to dinner with Austin. There was really nothing to do but laugh at herself, because, no, it was not Tim's fault. It was all her own.

But now, working with Austin was sure to be uncomfortable. She'd talk to him. Explain. Tell him it was just too fast for her. That wasn't a lie. *Says the girl who had planned out a life with a guy she'd never even met.* She'd have dived in head-first with Tim, if she'd had just the tiniest invitation.

CHAPTER 11

The barn was dark, and the horses started yelling at her as soon as she turned on the lights. A couple of particularly demanding equines banged their doors. It was strange; like they hadn't eaten already.

She couldn't be sure, but, looking at the feed cart, she swore there wasn't enough missing for them to have been fed breakfast. It was best to check before throwing more grain at them, though. Because there wasn't a good reason Austin wouldn't have done it, unless he'd forgotten to set his alarm and overslept. Or died in his sleep. Now that would be awkward.

She sent him a text. *You okay? Horses are acting like they haven't been fed.*

She picked up the feed scoop, making sure the metal connected with grain for that unmistakable sound. A torrent of whinnies filled the aisle. Definitely suspicious. If she didn't hear back from him shortly, she'd drive to Austin's cottage — better to leave the horses hungry for a while longer than feed them twice. Maybe he had food intoxication from something he'd eaten, though nothing last night had been suspect. She was about to return to her car when the phone chimed with a message.

Go ahead without me. I won't be in.

She stared at the screen a beat before typing, *Are you sick?*

Austin's answer came immediately. *Nope.*

Where are you?

At the border.

WHAT?? Border? What was he talking about? She jabbed at the call icon and waited for it to connect. The horses rumbled in one ear while the ringing trilled in the other. *Pick up, you...* oh, the names she had for him right now.

"Hi Emilie."

"What do you mean you're at the border?" She might have been screeching, because the horses stopped their complaining temporarily.

"What it sounds like. There's a lineup. At six AM. I don't get it."

"What I don't get is... why are you at the border? The US-Canadian border?"

"Lewiston, yep."

"But — what are you doing there?" He'd better have a good reason for this insane development, like maybe a sick relative.

"On my way to Florida."

"Florida? Austin — you mean you're deserting me? No notice or anything? Seriously?"

"I was talking to my ex last night after I got home. The trainer she's with needs help. There's a job waiting for me down there. No more pushing snow. And I'm tired of your whole princess act. She wants to get back together. Have a nice winter, Emilie."

And he hung up.

He hung up.

That...

Augh! And she'd forgotten to ask him about the horses, though she could guess the answer. She sent a text wondering if she'd even get a response. *Did you feed, by any sane chance?*

Nope.

She wanted to throw the phone at the floor, but it wasn't the phone's fault. This couldn't be happening. Obviously, last night's version of Austin had been an act; one she'd fallen for. It stung to feel so played; like he'd been waiting until she was on her own here, thinking she'd give him what he wanted because she had no choice. She should probably count her blessings that he'd managed things while she was away, even if that was part of his ploy. Make her feel complacent. Make her trust him. Then, as soon as an easier spot came along, book. If he'd blackmailed her, it wouldn't have changed her reaction last night — she didn't go for that — but at least she would have had some warning.

The horse next to where she stood rattled his door insistently.

"All right, all right." She tucked the phone back into a pocket and rolled out the cart, doling out morning grain until all the barn's inhabitants were satisfied.

I can't believe this.

But there was no time to feel sorry for herself; there were other horses to feed. She headed to the next barn.

The stallions were downright grumpy by the time she made it as far as them because normally they were first, being closest to Austin's cottage. She growled at them to back off as she pushed into their stalls to dump feed in their tubs, then sat on a bucket of supplements in the feed room to wait until they finished eating to turn them out, her mind racing.

The help got here at seven. Two of them were off today. Sundays were usually a light day, and Austin helped muck, then took Mondays off. How could he have deserted her? Who did that? Stupid question. It was just such a shock, because he hadn't seemed unhappy here. It was a pretty posh job as far as employment in the horse industry went, with benefits and a house. Apparently, winter in Florida with his willing ex was more appealing. If she'd let anything happen last night, she'd bet his true colours would have shone through eventually, anyway. Just another reminder to listen to her gut.

Just Lucky, the younger of the two stallions, was full of himself on a good day, let alone a sharp winter morning when his breakfast had been delayed. She didn't apologize for putting the chain in his mouth, snapping it to the back ring on the off side. He wasn't tall, but he outweighed and out-atti-tude-ed her by several units. She needed the advantage that shank arrangement would give her to get him out safely. He pranced next to her, barely contained, and when she released him he spun, tearing along the fenceline, stopping for some airs above the ground before he dropped and rolled. A faint glow warmed the horizon in the east, behind the tall trees, all pretty pinks and blues. She wanted to stop and appreciate it, but there would be no time for that today.

As she went back for the other stallion, Starway, she thought of Jay, missing him. This was where he'd lived until he'd started back into proper racehorse training. He was probably heading out to the track under the same indigo sky with Nate at this moment — because while her sister had come far enough to agree to a wedding, taking an actual honeymoon was something else altogether. It was just several degrees warmer, where they were.

Just to convince herself this wasn't a bad dream, before getting back in the car to help turn out the rest of the horses, she went to the manager's cottage. The door was unlocked, the smooth knob turning in her hand. She flipped on the lights.

The front closet was empty. The cupboards weren't, but he obviously hadn't been worried about that. There was food in the fridge, too, which she'd have to clean out before it looked like a microbiology project gone wrong. No clothes left in the bedroom. Yep. He was gone.

She'd have to call Liv. She didn't want to do anything to disrupt what should be a happy time for her sister, but how could she not tell her about this? Later, though.

None of the staff had arrived yet when she returned to the training barn. What if they stood her up too? Like they'd all gotten together and planned it out. *What could we do to finally push Emilie* — stable Emilie, who everyone thought had it all together — *over the edge?*

The flash of headlights outside caught her eye, and she sighed. At least someone was going to show up. Jillian walked in the end of the barn, closing the door behind her to keep out the pre-dawn chill, and Emilie almost raced over and hugged her.

"I have never been so happy to see anyone in my entire life." A crazy little laugh escaped from her throat. Exaggeration? Not sure.

Jillian loosened the scarf at her neck. "What's up?"

"Austin's not here."

"So let's go drag him out of bed." Jillian's lips pinched and twisted in a half-smile, half grimace, that made Emilie think Austin had been caught sleeping in before. "He couldn't wait one more day till his day off to get cast somewhere?"

"No, he's gone. Let's get these horses out, okay? Then I'll tell you what I know." She heard another car pull up.

"Ava," Jillian said.

"Thank goodness."

Ava, a high school student who helped on weekends, appeared shortly with a tray of Tim Horton's coffees. She stopped, looking from Jillian to Emilie. "Good morning! Hi Emilie!"

She still looked unsure as she came closer. Fair; Emilie wasn't usually standing in the aisle with a rope shank in her hands this time of morning, though it wasn't unusual for her to be here. Normally, she'd just be finishing up with Reba.

"Hi Ava. Austin's — not here this morning, so you're stuck with me," she explained.

"I'll take you over Austin any day." Ava smirked, breezing by to set the coffees in the tack room that doubled as their break room.

Emilie raised her eyebrows at Jillian, and Jillian gave a smirk of her own. So Austin wasn't a favourite with these girls. *She should have listened to her gut.*

"The stallions are already out. I'll go do Claire and Chique when we've taken care of the others. They'll be good and mad at me for being late."

The inhabitants of this barn — racehorses and yearlings — all behaved as the three of them walked them to their respective paddocks. The weanlings were another story. Only recently having come off feral mode, living outside since they'd been separated from their mothers, leading wasn't their strongpoint. Thankfully, there weren't a lot of them. Everyone got where they needed to be — fillies in one paddock, colts in another with babysitter Twizzle.

"All right. I'll put out the royalty and get those stalls done."

"You're not going to join us for coffee?" Jillian looked vaguely slighted. "You are helping us muck today, right?"

"Of course."

"So there's plenty of time for coffee."

You have time, maybe. But she didn't want to insult the only help she had. She'd already driven Austin away. "Okay. I'll be back."

Claire was more tolerant of the disrupted schedule than Chique. Emilie put the big mare out first, after doing a quick visual check. Her udder was beginning to fill, with just over three weeks to her due date. Claire was at the point in her gestation that made Emilie nervous. She didn't have Liv's experience. She could identify a mare in labour, but hadn't developed an eye for the subtle early warning signs in the days and hours leading up to that. Liv didn't need milk test strips or a foaling monitor to narrow the delivery's expected window. But even Liv admitted mares could fool you; changes could happen quickly. At this stage the fetus was viable, should Claire decide to foal unexpectedly early — like Chique's mom had done. The difference was, Sotisse had been past the magical date of January first. If Claire had her baby now, Liv would freak out. No one in the Thoroughbred world wanted a Christmas baby that, a week later, would, according to Jockey Club rules, be a year old.

Get a grip, Em. She was imagining worst-case scenarios left, right and centre. That was Liv's department. Or had been.

Chique pranced out much like her sire, Just Lucky had, and Emilie waited for the animated filly to settle. After her usual Dance of the Goblins — to which Claire gave merely an ear-flick and roll of one wall-eye — the two of them politely nibbled hay, nose to nose, and Emilie let herself pause to take a breath.

It was getting light enough that the photo she snapped with her phone would turn out. She could send it to Liv during the coffee break. The side-view Emilie shared each morning gave her sister a point of comparison for the expectant mare's changing shape — which would be more of an indication of the foal's imminent arrival than the calendar. Emilie studied the image, trying to see what Liv would see. Still round, both her rump and her belly. Claire's pelvis hadn't begun to adjust to prepare for the foal's arrival yet.

She left her car there and walked back to the training barn in an attempt to slow herself down while satisfying her need to keep moving. Made herself walk when she wanted to run. There was just so much to do, and this turn of events put everything in jeopardy. It was all fine for the farm staff to make Sunday an easy day, but Emilie didn't have that option. She wanted to finish stalls and be done; bring the horses in early; move on to the next ball in the air.

She had to call Liv. She needed to get that over with. She could do that as she walked. But when she dialed, she got voice mail. She tried again before she entered the training barn, with the same result. Liv must be out on a set. *Call me,* Emilie texted. Best not to send the photo of Claire right after that, because Liv would no doubt think something was wrong with the mare.

Someone had already backed the tractor and spreader into the barn, ready to be loaded. Inside the tack room, it was cosy, the small space filled with the slightly bitter smell of Tim's coffee that made Emilie long to be sitting in Triple Shot with a cappuccino. Faye wouldn't be looking for her yet. Not on a Sunday morning.

"Do you always stop for coffee after turning out?" She worked a cup free from the tray, not caring right now where it came from. Tim Horton's was high octane and she needed that more than something that actually tasted good.

Neither Jillian nor Ava looked apologetic. "Yes. It's Sunday mode."

The coffee was still warm, and with cream and sugar to smooth out the acidity, it was tolerable. "Who started that?"

Jillian shrugged. "It's been that way since I was hired." Which had been at least two years ago.

"Huh." She'd thought she knew what went on around this

place, but it was apparent she did not. If they liked her better than Austin, and Austin was okay with this, she'd have to keep her mouth shut. She thought of the book full of notes she'd left — the one he'd no doubt ignored — and wished she had something like that herself. She could use a manual right about now.

Emilie couldn't remember who the manager had been two years ago. She'd have to ask Kyrie tomorrow, because she'd been on staff for as long as Emilie could remember. She'd worked with Geai. Had this been his introduction? Emilie hadn't been very involved with the farm in those days. Not like Liv, who had been his shadow, soaking up every drop of information he'd given her. Emilie had known him more as a grandfather figure, a substitute for the one she'd never had. They'd always invited him to family dinners, Geai warming up every gathering with his generous smile and endless stories. He was woven into the fabric of this farm, and their lives. His death hadn't changed that.

"So, are you going to tell us what happened to Austin?" Jillian asked, crossing her long legs at the ankles.

Emilie couldn't sit down. And she called out Liv on never being able to relax. Her sister was officially better at it than she was now. She'd probably be lying on the beach this afternoon with Nate.

Should she mention the dinner? Would they judge her for the way the date with Austin had ended? Maybe it would be good to get some opinions from outside of her usual circle, without doing a google search. But her phone came to life and got her out of answering, at least for now. It was Liv.

"Sorry, I have to take this." She ducked back out into the barn aisle, feeling a wash of relief. Not that Liv could do anything. Emilie just felt better telling her.

The news shocked Liv and made Nate furious, launching

him into full-on overprotective mode. Emilie took some satisfaction imagining him running into Austin in Florida. She was pretty sure Nate could take Austin, even though he was probably fifty pounds lighter. Not that Nate would actually do anything. Would he?

She spent most of the call assuring Liv she was fine. She'd handle it. She had to, didn't she? This was her job this winter, though it was supposed to be overseeing things, not filling in for jerks who left others in a lurch right before Christmas.

After the call ended, she returned to the warm room and snatched up her coffee cup. "Let's get these stalls started. I can't sit still right now."

Jillian and Ava followed her out. "You're not getting out of telling us what happened," Jillian said, passing out pitchforks and brooms.

Emilie glugged the remainder of her coffee and tossed the cup in the garbage. "I got here this morning to ride Reba, and the horses told me they hadn't been fed. I thought he must be sick or have overslept. I texted him — and he was at the border. He's on his way to Florida."

"What?" Jillian gaped.

Ava gasped. "That rat! The nerve!"

"Yeah. Apparently he was talking to his ex last night. She's taking him back, and he's going to work for her boss." Who could blame him? That opportunity was more attractive than winter in Canada.

She could. She was totally blaming him.

That was enough information for them, for now. Emilie took her broom and fork to a stall and started sifting through bedding. She didn't mind mucking out. It was part mindless, part art, and once she tuned out Jillian and Ava's steady chatter — which didn't usually require her participation — she started to work through things. With five days till Christmas, Reba could have the rest of the year off. If she found the time to take Sylvie hacking again, that would be enough work for the filly until January when the racehorses and yearlings — who would be officially two — started up again. She only had three and a half days left at the clinic. Could she get out of that somehow? Ugh. So not a good thing to ask. And it made her sick to think of letting down Faye.

"You're making us look bad, Emilie!"

Ava's sing-song voice broke through, and Emilie glanced around. She was doing two to their one.

"Can one of you move this thing?" She wasn't even sure she remembered how to drive the tractor. It was on the list of things horse girls should know, but she'd failed to make it a priority. There had always been someone else.

Jillian nodded and climbed into the seat, moving this and that until it chugged to life. She must've backed it in, too. Impressive.

Her phone buzzed just as she was getting started again and disrupted her rhythm. It was Faye. *See you at noon?* She must have a sixth sense, because she assumed on Sundays that's when Emilie would be there. She wasn't anywhere close to being late yet.

She called, because in this case it would be more efficient than a text. "I'm not going to make it, Faye. I'm so sorry."

"Is everything okay at the farm?"

"Yes, and no. Austin bailed, so we're short-handed."

"What do you mean, Austin bailed?"

"He's gone."

"Gone?"

She couldn't blame Faye for her confusion; she hadn't quite worked through her own. "Yeah. AWOL. On his way to Florida, apparently."

"Like... out of the blue?"

Not exactly. "If you're still there when I can get away from here, I'll come by and bring you up to speed."

"Well, if you need anything, call Dean. You've helped him out enough times with hay. I'm sure he'd be glad to step up. I'm definitely going to need the full scoop!"

Ava claimed they finished the training barn in record time, and she and Emilie walked while Jillian dumped the spreader and met them at the broodmare barn. At ten o'clock, both Jillian and Ava stopped mucking and set aside their forks like they were responding to some alarm clock Emilie hadn't heard.

"Coffee break," Ava said.

"Another one? First coffee and second coffee?"

Don't complain, Emilie. You need these two. She followed them back to the training barn. There was another car parked there when they arrived, and Emilie recognized it on the spot. It belonged to Will.

"What are you doing here?" she asked as he climbed out. "Aren't you supposed to be in the city?"

"I heard you had an emergency," he said, and leaned back in, producing a tray of coffees from the café and a white paper bag.

"You are a saint," Emilie said, attaching herself to him.

Will laughed and balanced the hot beverages until she released him. "I'll help Faye this afternoon. You don't have to worry about her. Take these. I'm heading back there."

"Thank you. And thank Faye. You two are the best."

"Let me know if you need any help around here tomorrow."

"What do you see yourself doing, exactly?" Emilie eyed him skeptically. She'd seen him throw around bales of hay, but didn't think he'd want to handle a horse.

"I can muck a stall. Ask Nate."

So after he drove away, she did, sending off a text, surprised when the response came quickly. *He can. Pretty well, even. But I'll need photos of Mr. Pastry Chef with a pitchfork in his hands.* It made her laugh.

"I guess we'll be well-caffeinated!" She carried the treasure to the coffee room, Ava and Jillian close behind, then passed out the cups. A proper cappuccino might be the thing that held her together today. And pastry. *Don't forget the pastry.*

"What's the rest of the Austin story, Emilie?" Jillian propped her legs up, thighs a perfect ninety degrees to her calves, coffee in one hand, croissant in the other. She had a sly twist to her lips.

Emilie sighed, slumping into one of the vacant chairs. "Please tell me I'm not the only one he's asked out."

Ava laughed, glancing at Jillian. "You're not. And he didn't care when I told him I was way too young for him."

"He thinks he's quite the ladies' man." Jillian rolled her eyes.

"I shouldn't be telling you guys this. I'm kind of your boss, right?"

"You're bonding with your staff," Jillian encouraged. Ava nodded.

Fine. "So, I may have had dinner with him last night." She deserved the laughter. She really did. "Mistake, right?"

"Please, go on," Jillian ejected between snorts, not trying nearly hard enough to get control. "I take it things did not go well?"

"They went fine for me. I just may have jumped out of the car when he tried to kiss me."

"He didn't even walk you to the door?" Ava gaped. "He totally deserved that reaction. What an idiot." Even a high school student thought Austin's behaviour was uncouth. That was validation.

What if he had walked her to the door? That would have been way worse. Way more awkward. "I'm the idiot."

"I do have to wonder what you were thinking," Jillian said, more composed now. "But you haven't been around him as much as us, so go easy on yourself."

"Thanks," she said, casting Jillian a self-conscious look. "Can we go back to work now?" The conversation, the caffeine, the situation; all of it was making her twitchy.

"Relax, Emilie," Jillian said. "Everything's under control."

Was it, though?

CHAPTER 12

The alarm jolted her out of a deep slumber, the abruptness of surfacing to consciousness giving her a splitting headache and sore muscles. She propped herself up and sneezed.

No. No, no, no. She could not get sick.

Yet, her throat felt chunky, her nose stuffed, her head clouded. This wasn't just lack of sleep. She sank back into her pillows.

She could just lie here. Keep staring up at the dark ceiling. Go back to sleep. She could tell them all she was sick. No one else had a day off, so the farm staff would get by as well as they had yesterday. Sam at the clinic would survive. She only worked a half-day today. If she called and left a message, Trudy would reschedule her appointments or reassign them — which meant more work for Sam. But Emilie had never taken a day off before, except to go to the wedding, so Sam would understand. It was Faye she felt bad about. So much work at the café right now. Lucy was still coming in to help when she could, but with her mom's health, it was hit or miss.

This is what she got for going away. Give her body's defences a few days off and a gleeful virus saw the opportunity to take her down. No, she would not stay in bed. She wasn't going down without a fight.

A steamy shower temporarily cleared her nasal passages and warmed her aching muscles, and she swallowed a handful of echinacea root capsules, even if that kind of felt like closing the barn door after the horse was out. *Please, please don't let there be any loose horses today.*

Then she looked out the window. It was snowing so hard the view was obliterated, ice crusted around the edges of the glass. How? How had she missed the forecast for a blizzard?

She reconsidered crawling back into bed. Snow day! Buses cancelled! She'd doze till it got light out; have a leisurely breakfast. That's why she was doing the physiotherapy internship. To have a normal life. Not this life. She'd consciously opted out of this life. And found herself tossed right back in. *You can run, but you can't hide.*

Then she laughed. Or cried. She couldn't tell. There was just a lot of snot, either way. She blew her nose, and the image of a cartoon she remembered seeing online came to her mind. *Someone pamper me! Oh yeah. I forgot. I'm a strong, independent woman. Shit.*

And there were horses to be fed.

That's me, living the meme.

She hopped into leggings and dragged a turtleneck over her messy hair. Because what was the point in brushing it before that happened? Then she braided the dark length and zipped on a hoodie. Her thermal socks came almost to her knees. Better make coffee now, because doing snow cleanup around the farm was going to take a while. The crew wouldn't be able to make it up the lane if it wasn't clear. She needed caffeine. Badly.

All she had was a little Keurig, which was fine. The machine warmed up, then she followed the prompts on the screen. That's what the tractor needed. Maybe the old beast had a manual online. She tried to recall the process; should have paid more attention to Jillian yesterday. There were two sticks. She could drive a standard transmission car; surely she could manage a tractor.

It felt wrong to bolt down the coffee, extracted from a lovely Irish Cream pod — with a dollop of actual Irish Cream for therapeutic purposes — but she needed to get out there. She alternated sips with bites of a Kashi bar, breakfast du jour, then set her mug in the sink to deal with later and loaded up on cold meds, not trusting her herbal go-to in this case. She shrugged into her old ski pants; pulled on an infinity scarf. Toque. Jacket. *Time to shine, Emilie.* Because, like Austin, the sun sure wasn't showing up today.

She loved winter, really she did. The snow was pretty — if you didn't have to go out and shovel it. She would feed the horses first. Snowshoes, maybe?

There was no sense taking her car out — the white stuff was up to her knees. By the time she reached Claire and Chique's barn, she was drenched in sweat and her head felt ready to explode. Those cold meds could kick in any time now.

Making the rounds, she ended up at the stallion barn. The tractor shed was at the front of the farm, right across from the office barn, so now she had a long walk back. The snow was heavy, so tiring to trudge through. But when she reached the lane that led past the training track, she realized it was ploughed. She stopped dead, looking around, as if the Angel Snow Removal person would reveal themselves. No one. Nothing but more snow, highlighted by the sulfur lamp, drifting down with purpose.

A miracle, and it wasn't even Christmas. She started

walking toward the office barn, being careful not to slip on the glassy surface under that fresh layer of white. There could really only be one person who would do this for her. She dug her phone out of her pocket and before opening the side door to the small stable, made a call, knowing he was up.

"Hey, Em." Dean's voice was warm.

"It was you, wasn't it?"

He chuckled. "I didn't do your whole farm, but your staff will be able to get in."

"I love you. Will you marry me?"

Thankfully, Dean just laughed again. "It was a joint decision," he said. "With Faye. So you'll have to take both of us."

"Done. So done. I love you both. Tell Will he's out of luck. He'll have to find someone else."

"Speaking of Will — there's no way he's getting into the city, so he's here to help too, if you need it."

"Faye will probably need him more. This morning will be a breeze over here. We've got one more person than we did yesterday."

She turned Chique and Claire out in the dark and cleaned their stalls to get them out of the way. Liv's photo of the day would have to wait. Then she remembered — her parents. She'd have to call them. There was no way she was going to Montreal now, with Austin gone. That settled it. Festive holidays with estranged relatives would have to wait.

I'll be home for Christmas. Even if no one else will.

BY THE TIME night check rolled around, she was seriously dragging. She could feel the cold virus invading her cells one by one, the medication ceasing to be effective. How was she ever going to get through tomorrow? Mind over matter, that was all there was to it. Well, that, and lots of caffeine.

Trudging from barn to barn on foot would keep her awake. Not that she couldn't do night check in her sleep, but driving the car in her state wasn't advisable. She looked up at the stars, bright flickering specks against an inky eternity. She'd get through. This too shall pass, right?

Claire and Chique were quiet, watching her, hoping she didn't know there wasn't grain at this feeding. She gave them more hay, topped their buckets up with warm water, and peeked at Claire's important parts with a flashlight. No drastic changes. That much was good. She wasn't staying up at night to watch the mare, but the camera was installed. Might as well get into the routine.

She'd have to do foal watch. That was supposed to be part of Austin's job. Unless she could find a farm manager soon. Like, yesterday would have been good, if she'd known yesterday what today held. There was just no way she could do night watch, and help during the day, and do her internship, and lend a hand at the café. Something had to go.

That something was going to have to be Faye. It wasn't that Faye wouldn't understand; it was just Emilie felt guilty leaving her with so much, when she'd been counting on the help. Just like Emilie had been counting on Austin. She'd bet Austin didn't feel the least bit guilty.

The training barn greeted her with the usual chorus. She stopped at Reba's stall after turning on the lights, slipping in for a moment to scratch the bright chestnut and offer up a peppermint.

"Well, there's a surprise. You ate every last piece of hay, didn't you?"

Some of these horses got grain at this feeding. She dished out their rations into small buckets and soaked them for a warm meal. Everyone got hay. Everyone got warm water. Twizzle banged on his door, ignoring the hay, because grain was life, obviously.

"And no matter how sweet a face you give me, sugar pants, you don't need any," she cooed at Reba. A bonus flake of second cut, rich with alfalfa, would have to do.

She didn't know why she made an extra pass down the barn before she planned to leave. The same reason people run back to check locks or make sure the stove is off. Twizzle wasn't at his feed tub. He'd gone right to it when she'd dumped his late meal in there. She'd left him nose-deep. But now he was standing, and a quick peek into the tub showed he hadn't licked it clean. He stretched out his neck, upper lip contorting in the air, but it wasn't humorous, combined with the other factors, and the tightening in her stomach. *Please, no. Please, please no.*

His head dropped, nose to the straw, and he pawed. *Just... no.* Stopped. Pawed, then held his foreleg up, flamingo-style, swinging it in the air. Then he flopped down where he was, rolled, and settled on his sternum with a moan, head circling to his side.

"Oh, buddy. All right."

Please don't be serious. Please don't make me have to call Liv and tell her that her old horse is trying to die. Please, please, please. She plunged a syringe full of air into the glass bottle and carefully drew up the Banamine so there were no bubbles, telling herself that a few seconds of patience now would save her more seconds later.

"On your feet, old man," she said, rolling the door open. Twizzle lay flat out now. "I know you're convinced you're dying. I'm going to give you a fresh outlook. Get up." She clucked, and the old racehorse in him responded, clambering to his feet.

He didn't bother to shake off the shavings; he just stood, looking baleful. Emilie guided him to the wall tie. *Okay Em, you know how to do this. You have done it before.* Just not for a while, and not often.

More points for the old racehorse in him, though he was probably uncomfortable enough not to protest — he stood like a champ as she prodded to find the jugular under his hairy coat, held the syringe at an angle and slipped in the needle, hoping she'd hit the vein. She pulled back on the plunger and sighed as red seeped in. Bingo. Even Twizzle let out a breath, like he was saying, *pretty good for an amateur, kid.* She rubbed his neck over the injection site with the heel of her hand and noted the time.

After she unsnapped him, Twizzle flopped back down, leaving Emilie's heart still in her throat. *It takes a few minutes to circulate.* And he was resting quietly, not rolling. If he'd do that, she wouldn't walk him. In the meantime, she wasn't going anywhere.

Nothing says Merry Christmas like a colicky horse.

She grabbed a muck bucket and fork and carefully removed his remaining hay from the corner. She took out his feed tub, dumping what remained of his unfinished snack and rinsing it out. She unhooked his water bucket, emptied it outside, then refilled it with warm water, ready for him if the drug did its thing.

When she got back with the bucket, he was standing at the door, ears perked, rumbling. *What did you do with my hay, woman?*

Magical, magical Banamine. After hanging the water, she threw her arms around his neck and pressed her cheek to his warm fuzz.

"Hate to tell you old man, but you're still not getting your hay back." Just in case it was an impaction somewhere in his intestinal tract.

She'd pick out the manure from his stall so she could monitor his future output. There was lots of it, anyway, and he'd drunk half his water bucket. Maybe it had been an ulcer thing, the way it had come on with eating. She couldn't remember if he was prone to such attacks. She didn't know enough about anything, coming in cold. She'd ask Liv — in the morning, if Twizzle continued to improve.

Of course, this episode meant she wasn't getting any sleep tonight. Even though he was once again bright and demanding food, she needed to keep an eye on him. Too bad she didn't have another camera, like the one in Claire's stall.

"I'll see you in an hour," she said, setting an alarm on her phone before walking down the aisle, looking in each and every stall before walking back to the house. She'd gather some things, pick up her car to drive around and finish night check, then camp out in the barn. At least she'd have lots of company here.

CHAPTER 13

The sand was warm; the ocean was blue. And Tim Miller was shirtless again.

"Emilie, wake up."

Her eyelids almost crackled as she pried them open, seeing Kyrie through a slit standing just inside the break room door. *Did I forget to set the alarm after my last check? And what is Tim doing in my dreams? Just no. Please, no.*

"What time is it?" Her words came out in a croak.

"Six. Have you fed?"

Emilie dragged herself upright, rubbing at her crusty lashes. "No. Damn. I'm sorry. I'll —"

"I've got it. Twizzle have one of his bouts?"

"He does that, does he?" She could wish all she wanted that she'd known, but again, this was not her usual gig. She was picking up these gems as she went. She should add them to her notes.

"Austin probably forgot to order his omeprazole. Twizzle lives on it." Kyrie clattered about through the cupboards, found a fat plastic bottle that looked like the kind the ulcer medication came in and shook it after checking the label. "Yep. Dregs."

"I'll pick some up for him from the vet. Do you usually feed on Austin's day off?"

"Yes. Pretty random you found Twizzle. Lucky for him. What were you doing out here that time of night?"

So, news hadn't spread that far. The farm wasn't the racetrack; these people were a distant part of that world. They didn't interact in the same way outside of work. This was their job, not their family, whereas the track was a big, dysfunctional one.

She stumbled into the aisle, going straight to Twizzle's stall. There were several healthy-looking piles of manure. She'd heard it said dog people didn't like cleaning up after dogs, but horse people loved doing stalls. "Love" might be a strong word, but that was why. Manure was life.

"He seems fine now," Kyrie said. "Think it's okay for him to have some breakfast?"

"I'll soak it for him and make it extra-sloppy."

Twizzle dove into his mush, slurping and smearing it around the tub. He licked it clean, and stared at her, looking short-changed.

"Sorry, buddy. You'll be back to your usual ration in no time." That reminded her to text the vet about picking up the omeprazole.

The break room called her back. Kyrie had started the coffee brewing, and the last drops were falling into the carafe. She poured herself a cup, adding lots of cream from the fridge to make it palatable, and guzzled it down. Then she'd just rest her head for a moment. The coffee would kick in and wake her up.

As it turned out, Kyrie woke her up again, with the rest of the staff for an audience. Ava was here this week because school was off until the new year. And she brought coffee again. Emilie didn't refuse another dose. The more the merrier.

"They told me about Austin. You don't need to be here, Em," Kyrie insisted. "You look like death warmed over."

"I do have to be at the clinic this morning." At eight. She'd have to fit in a shower. Did she have time to pick up some cookies and squares to take with her to distract Trudy? Because she was going to be late. She could call ahead to Faye. Maybe best to order cappuccinos for Trudy and Sam too, just in case. Smooth over any possible discord. Better leave now. "Thanks, all of you. Call me if you need me."

En route to the café it hit her — with everything going on, she'd forgotten she still hadn't heard from the Golden Retriever breeder about Theo. As soon as she had a spare minute, she'd call them. She dashed in and out of Triple Shot with only a wave and mumbled thanks to Faye, because there wasn't time for more. Faye was too busy with customers to talk, anyway.

There was a tree in the clinic's waiting room, with fake presents — and what did she know, maybe some real ones — under it. Of course, the tree was fake too. These days, with allergies and fire codes, you couldn't have a natural tree in a place of business. Trudy smiled cordially when she handed the office manager the fancy coffee and raised the package of cookies and squares. She needed all the brownie points she could collect this week. One and a half more days and the clinic would be closed for the holidays, and she'd have one less place she had to be. Farm plus café seemed manageable by comparison.

Her giddy state of over-tired was serving her well today. She was maybe too cheerful, but this time of year no one noticed. All she had to do was keep moving. If she fell asleep on the job here, she'd be in trouble. She couldn't afford to screw this up. She needed it to graduate. She hadn't come this far to fail. The last two days had been a reminder.

It was lunchtime before she had the chance to call the Golden breeder. In her hurry, she'd forgotten to bring something proper to eat, so she was sneaking cookies from the treats she'd brought, and helping herself to a box of chocolates a patient had gifted them. She couldn't really taste them because of her cold, but the sugar would help keep her going.

It took a moment for the breeder to remember who she was. "Oh yes! I'm sorry, I've just been so busy interviewing potential puppy buyers, I forgot to call you. Theo's family has decided to keep him. They've started working with a trainer who is really helping them."

"I understand." She tried not to sound as downcast as she felt. That was what was best for Theo, probably. But it seemed like another straw to Emilie.

"I still have a couple of puppies from this litter available though, if I can tempt you."

"As much as I would love one," she said, deflated, "I couldn't manage a puppy right now. Thank you, though." She probably had no business taking on a six-month-old, for that matter, but she would have found the time, somehow. It would be so worth it. She asked the breeder to keep her in mind should another older dog become available, and disconnected.

"Emilie? Are you okay?"

She straightened at the sound of Sam's voice, putting away her phone, and ran her hands over her hair. Her nose dripped despite the decongestant she'd taken and she reached for a tissue. "I'm fine. I just had a long night. The manager at the farm quit, and I was up with a sick horse."

"You should have told me. I could have managed."

"I'm okay, really."

"Emilie. You can go home."

"But —"

"Go home. It's all right. Get some rest." Sam's words were kind, but her eyes were insistent. "Call me tomorrow, and if you're still not feeling well, you don't have to come in. We've already had two cancellations. Everyone's schedules go haywire this time of year. We'll find a way to make up your hours after the holidays."

Emilie nodded, and said, "Thanks." But she didn't feel grateful.

SHE WASN'T one who felt sorry for herself. She always kept her head above water, kept a positive attitude. But tonight she was going to let herself have a good, old-fashioned sulk. With wine and macaroni and cheese and ice cream. Kyrie was doing night check, so she was totally free to mope.

Emilie's always got it together. I don't know how she does everything she does. Emilie never falls apart. It's okay for Liv to be messed up. Even Nate's allowed to be messed up. *But not Emilie.* Not ever.

But Emilie's done. She's done being the stable one. It's her turn to fall apart.

She'd never been able to find any science to support her theory that wine fought the cold virus, but it made sense. Hundred-proof rum would probably be a better bet — the higher the alcohol content, the better. Maybe she should ditch physiotherapy and get another degree. What program would she have to be in to study something like that? Surely she could get a grant for that research. Then she could be like Sylvie, married to her lab.

She'd rather have a Lab.

This was as much romance as she was going to get right

now, watching saccharine-sweet Hallmark Christmas movies. It was for the best. They might not seem like a dose of reality, but they were. Because this was the only place Happily Ever After would exist for her — in the frames of these films and the pages of the novels she read.

A dog was a better — safer — choice. Dogs didn't let you down. But finding a dog was proving to be easier said than done. Rescue dogs were a commodity right now. At least those from reputable sources. Horses were great, but they couldn't sleep on your bed or curl up next to you in front of the TV.

She clicked away during the commercials because she wasn't organized enough to set up the PVR these days. *That's right, Emilie is not organized right now.* She stopped at CBC to check the hockey games on tonight — not following the schedule closely; she had to bring herself up to speed. The Leafs were playing Ottawa, tied one-all in the second period. Montreal was on the road out west — oh, look, in Calgary tonight. She wondered if Tim was in the lineup. The Canadiens better win that one. She might have to stay awake long enough to watch, like her doing so would better their chances. The wine was making her sleepy, though.

When she woke up, she was disoriented for a moment. It must be late — there was an infomercial on the screen now. She hadn't been able to stay awake for the Hallmark movie's Happily Ever After, let alone the hockey game. She dragged herself to her bed, and hoped the worst of this cold would be behind her by the morning.

CHAPTER 14

It was never a surprise when they got a good turnout at the café for an unplugged night, but each time she saw the place packed with people, Emilie's face glowed. Tonight, though, it made her a little sad. It was Christmas Eve-Eve. She missed Liv and Nate because they weren't here, and it felt like they should be.

"You're dead on your feet, girl."

"I'm fine. Just don't let me sit down!" She shook off Faye's concern, even though it was true. Working in the sub-zero temperatures all day wiped her out. Less than adequate sleep didn't help. And she was still fighting this cold. That was twice in twelve hours someone had referred to her appearance in some way related to death. Maybe she should listen.

She had let Sam talk her into staying home today — the comment *plus, we really don't want you making any of our patients sick* was the clincher. That hadn't stopped her from helping around the farm, though. The thing about a bad head cold was, it always felt so much worse when you stayed indoors. Being outside, moving around, helped clear her head more than the cold remedies did, even if it meant she was blowing her nose every five minutes. Her poor, red, nose.

After a hot shower, which helped to drain her sinuses even more, she'd felt like she'd turned the corner with this virus. She wasn't constantly sniffling. One more good sleep would go a long way to putting it behind her. But she wasn't missing tonight, no way. Even if she was drained.

She couldn't escape Faye's scowl before her friend handed her a tray of goodies. "Don't drop it, or I'll have to send you home."

That wasn't going to happen. She was seeing this through. She just needed more caffeine and was in just the place to get some — after she'd set all the tables up with their treats. Coffees had already been served.

One of the other band members — the band from which Nate was missing, with his Florida departure — joined Will tonight. He wasn't as good as Nate, but Will had an appealing voice and Josh did a nice job of harmonizing. The thing about Christmas songs, too, was that many of the patrons joined in. They did a varied selection of carols and secular songs. It gave the café such a nice, cosy feeling; one befitting the season. Emilie dashed away thoughts of how different her Christmas was going to be again. How different life from here on in would be.

With the year drawing to a close, it was easy to jump ahead to thoughts of "out with the old, in with the new." She felt like there should be big goals. No resolutions, because what would she change? *I resolve to focus on one thing and not be spread thin over several.* Because would that ever happen? She caught Faye watching her again. She didn't want to give this up, helping at the café. Faye relied on her. But something in her life had to change.

She made herself sing along in an attempt to keep herself

alert. *Let it snow, let it snow, let it snow.* She'd had quite enough snow for a little while, if she was honest with herself. She wasn't being very honest with herself about much right now, so she just sang louder.

Half an hour into their performance, Emilie spotted Sylvie by the door. She waved, and Sylvie smiled and made her way over, skirting around the edges of the tables. After Emilie delivered the platter in her hand, she met Sylvie with a hug.

"I'm so happy you made it! Want something to drink?"

"Do you do decaf anything?"

"We certainly do."

She made the drink herself, and even managed a heart pattern when she poured the milk. She was getting better at them. It was especially impressive, given her current state of exhaustion.

"Here you go. And you have to have a Nanaimo bar. Seasonal special." She set one of the squares on a plate. "How's your mom doing?"

"Pretty well. The first round of chemo is finished. She's tired, of course, but feeling a little better." Sylvie bit into the square. "Delicious," she mumbled, then looked apologetic for talking with food in her mouth. "What about you? I heard your manager quit?"

"Yes. Fine timing."

"Now is when you really need to put me to work."

"We're okay at the farm, really. The three workers we have are solid, and one of the weekend helpers is around this week, too. They're efficient. It just shows how little Austin really did." She'd add the whole Austin story to the There Needs To Be Wine list.

"I can't do your internship for you, but I could help here. I can bake and load a dishwasher. I mean it, Emilie. My mother keeps shooing me away. She says I'm hovering and I'm making her crazy."

Emilie laughed — and thought the timing couldn't be any more perfect. "I'll talk to Faye tomorrow morning. There's a little too much going on tonight." If she could offer Sylvie in her place, she'd feel less guilty about telling Faye she was going to have to give up being at the café so much.

Sylvie didn't stay long, Emilie sending her on her way with more treats for Roger and Hélène. There was a lull in her need to serve people, and she pounced on the espresso shot Faye reluctantly offered, taking it to a vacant table in the corner, out of the way, with the Nanaimo bar she'd snatched. One bite of sweet, one sip of bitter. Sweet, bitter. Bittersweet. Like everything tonight.

The tried-and-true espresso and sugar combo was failing her. The music, the soft singing, the warm room... she couldn't keep her head up. She pushed the dishes aside and rested her head on her arms. She had to close her eyes. Just for a moment.

IT WAS TOO QUIET. It was nice, though. *Oh... no.*

She sat up quickly. The room was empty, save for Faye, Will and Josh, sitting at a nearby table. Faye's arms were crossed, eyebrows raised, gaze firmly attached to Emilie.

"Welcome back," she said.

Emilie stumbled to her feet, but had to take a few seconds to steady herself. "Why didn't you wake me up? Gah, I'm so embarrassed." She snatched up the espresso cup and empty plate and flew into the kitchen.

She wasn't really surprised when Faye was right behind her. "You need to go home and get some sleep, but I don't trust you to drive. I'm done here, so I'll take you."

"I'm fine."

"You are not, Emilie. And you won't be doing any of us any favours if you drive into a ditch, or worse. So shut up and come along. You're being frustratingly like your sister, do you know that?"

Ouch. That hurt. They weren't the same, not really. Emilie knew how to have fun. She knew how to relax. She knew how... to... ask... for...

Help.

"Sorry, Faye. Thanks. I'm ready to go."

Faye dropped her off with stern instructions to go to bed. Once the black Corolla disappeared — and that meant following the lights all the way down the lane for as far as she could see it, which was pretty far this time of year when the trees were bare of leaves — she sneaked out. Who was she sneaking from? Silly girl.

But her car was at Triple Shot. Well... easy solution. Liv and Nate had driven the farm truck and trailer to Florida, so Liv's Nissan was in the garage. She ducked back inside, found the keys, and took Liv's car to do one more check on the horses, because after the way things had been going this week, she didn't trust them not to throw another curve ball at her.

The exercise woke her back up. The little power nap had refreshed her a tiny bit. Despite her paranoia, all the horses were quietly munching hay, or napping, or playing with stall toys. Twizzle had cleaned his late feed and was nose-deep in a flake of alfalfa. The weanlings were mostly all lying down, reformed from their temporary wild ways and enjoying having soft beds on the wintry nights. Chique and Claire demanded peppermints. Claire didn't look as if she was going to do anything crazy like foal early.

She parked the Nissan back in the garage and went straight up to her bedroom, changing into her pyjamas before brushing her teeth. Crawling gratefully into bed, one pillow under her head, her arms wrapped around another, she let herself sink into the welcoming mattress.

But... sleep didn't come. Fine time for that espresso shot to activate. Tomorrow was going to be even longer.

So, she got up, went downstairs, and started pulling ingredients from the cupboards. She'd thought doing so much baking at the café might make her sick of it, but such was not the case. And it was never wrong to do more baking at Christmas. She plugged her phone into the speakers and hit play on the list of songs she'd been adding to in the last few weeks.

Nate would be proud of the diversity of her holiday tune selection. Somehow, beautiful hymns didn't fit her mood. Then she mixed and rolled and cut and danced around the kitchen, singing along to "A Fairytale of New York" and "I Will Be Hating You For Christmas" (in honour of Austin) and a punk version of "Twelve Days of Christmas" until the last sheet was out of the oven. Then she turned the stove off, cued up Joni Mitchell's "River," and at last fell asleep on the living room couch.

CHAPTER 15

Gus curled up on his dog bed near the fire, looking like part of a Christmas card, golden light on a Golden Retriever with a filter of red and white sparkles from the tree. Emilie's nose had cleared enough to smell all the amazingness Faye was whipping up: turkey and savoury dressing and a cinnamony apple pie. The rich scent of the real Balsam Fir, decorated with Faye's impeccable taste, made her feel as if she was wandering through the woods, though she was grateful for the warmth of the Taylors' living room. She'd been spending enough time out in the cold this week.

She didn't know why Faye had decided to do Christmas dinner on Christmas Eve, but she was happy to be here just the same. She'd take all the holiday spirit she could get with these people, sipping rich rummy eggnog while they waited for the bird to be ready.

"I've got some news," Will said from the couch, one arm draped over Faye's shoulders. Faye leaned into him, her legs tucked under her.

Emilie's mouth popped open, and she searched Faye's hands. Faye shook her head slightly and rolled her eyes. No, not that. No ring.

Emilie frowned — she'd been sure after Nate and Liv's wedding their engagement would be imminent — but set aside her disappointment. "So? Let's hear it."

"I'm done at the restaurant."

"What?" It wasn't an engagement announcement, but that was possibly the next best thing. Will hated working at the fancy restaurant in the city — one he'd been at for years. It must mean the café was doing well enough to provide him with a sustainable income. "That's great!"

"He's going to be around All. The. Time," Faye said with mock exasperation.

"If you get sick of him at the café, just send him over to the farm." Emilie grinned.

"You holding up okay, Em?" Dean asked. "Really?"

"It's been a rough week, but I got through it because of you guys and the incredible staff. I literally could not have without that. Thank you."

"You'd do — have done — the same for us," Dean replied. "We're happy to help."

Faye ducked out from under Will's arm, unfolding her legs and standing. "Speaking of help, I could use some in the kitchen. It's just about time."

Emilie imagined her parents in Montreal having the traditional Christmas Eve tourtière and wondered what Liv might be experiencing with Nate's family in Calgary. Connie Miller was very much a mother hen, so she imagined there would be no shortage of food. It would be a hard holiday for them this year too, because the oldest son and his wife had been killed in a car accident in the spring. It put her own woes in perspective.

Her mind drifted to Tim, and her heart softened toward him. He'd be missing his brother, too.

Dean poured the wine, and Will and Emilie set the side dishes on the table while Faye cut the turkey. They ate in the kitchen, even though there was a dining room. Emilie had never seen Faye use that room, or her parents' dinner and silverware.

Everything was wonderful, because Faye cooked as well as she baked. They all helped her clear the table when the meal was done. Will was washing dishes, Dean brewing coffee, and Faye slicing pie when Emilie's phone rang. She stared at the number, eyebrows raised as she recognized it.

"Sorry — I have to take this." She swiped it open and pressed it to her ear. "Hello?"

"Could I speak to Emilie, please?"

"Yes! Speaking."

"Emilie, it's Norma."

"Merry Christmas, Norma!"

"Yes, Merry Christmas. I'm sorry to bother you on Christmas Eve, but… well, let me get right to it. One of the dogs we bred, a three-year-old female, is in need of a foster situation. Her owner just passed away and the family isn't able to keep her, so of course we said we'd take her back. But the kennel is so full this time of year, we really have no space for her. Is it at all possible you might be able to keep her over the holidays?"

"Yes!" she said, almost over top of Norma's words. "Of course! Where is she? Do you want me to come right now?"

"Could you do that? It would mean so much. She's with us. They dropped her off this afternoon."

"I'll be there in half an hour."

She disconnected and squealed, rushing for her coat. Her

excitement roused Gus, and the Golden bounded into the room, barking. "I'm so sorry, but I've got to go pick up a dog!"

"Wait!" Faye stopped her in her tracks, holding up a finger with one hand while she rifled through a cupboard with the other. She produced a small plastic container. "Take a piece of pie with you."

Emilie laughed. "Of course. Thanks, Faye!" Without any more explanation, she raced out of the house to her car.

The roads were dry, but she tried to convince herself to keep her speed moderate. Just like her first visit, Labradors bombarded her as Norma let her in the house, a mix of blacks, yellows, chocolates, though she didn't know if it was exactly the same as last time. What colour was her dog? What was her name? Was she one of these? *Her dog.* She'd agreed to foster. Maybe they wouldn't think she was a suitable forever home.

"Thank you so much for coming. I think it would over-whelm poor Holly, staying with us right now. The kennel can be quite noisy when we're full, and the house is crowded, as you can probably tell. She lived with an elderly woman, so her life was rather sedate."

"Where is she?" Emilie could barely contain herself.

"Let me just put these hooligans away for a moment." With that, Norma ushered the exuberant pack into another room and closed the doors. After a few barks and some whining, they settled. "There. Come this way."

There was a mud room at the back of the house with two plastic kennels. Tails thumped and there was more whining and lolling tongues, dark noses pressed to the door grills.

"Here she is."

Norma released the occupant of the end crate, and a small black Lab squirmed out. Her body swayed more than her tail wagged, the big brown eyes that looked up at Emilie melting her heart in an instant. Emilie crouched down and the dog was immediately in her face, though remarkably polite about it.

"She's beautiful. What did you say her name was?"

"Holly."

"What a perfect name." For her Christmas dog.

"She was born on Christmas Day. We had holiday names for the whole litter. Now, let me gather what you need. Charles, can you collapse the crate? You don't have a crate, do you, Emilie?"

"No, I don't."

"I know this was a surprise. The family left her food and a bag of her toys and bowls and such. The poor thing. Of course I feel bad for the family, too. They feel terrible about not being able to take her themselves," Norma added. "Here's her leash. I don't know how well trained she is, so best to keep her on it until you've spent some time with her."

Emilie couldn't help a little smile as she accepted the royal blue nylon lead and snapped it to Holly's matching collar. Dog people were not so unlike horse people, putting their thoughts for the animals before humans sometimes.

Holly hopped willingly into the back seat while Norma placed the kennel and supplies in the hatch.

"Thank you again, Emilie. We'll talk again soon. If you have any questions or need anything else, let me know. I don't think it will take long to place this girl, but the timing, you know. Everyone's so busy."

"You're welcome," she said, meaning it entirely. And she hoped they had, in fact, just sent Holly to her new home. But she didn't want to get her hopes up.

Holly was quiet as she drove, but Emilie couldn't help a steady stream of dialogue. She hoped Holly understood her sentiment, if not her words. "You poor sweet girl, having your world turned upside down. I'm happy you have a great breeder, though. So in a way, you're pretty lucky. And I'm lucky they called me."

She didn't know why they had. She must've made a good impression on her first visit, but if they had a waiting list, she probably wasn't at the top of it. Maybe they'd called others on that list already. Before she was home, she'd decided: in the morning she'd call and ask them if Holly could stay. She serenaded Holly with carols the rest of the way home.

Leaving Holly in the car while she dragged the crate inside and set it up, she made a second trip for the dog bed and supplies. Then she came back to that mournful face in the vehicle's window.

"You didn't think I'd leave you out here, did you?" Emilie snapped the lead on and waited while Holly hopped out, giving her a moment outside before showing her the house.

She was so mild-mannered. At three years old, Emilie expected Holly was responsible in the house and dragged the dog bed up to her room, flopping it on the floor between her own bed and the wall. Holly climbed onto it and dropped into its softness, resting her head on her front paws.

"Aren't you the perfect little Labrador? My Christmas angel." She changed into her PJs and climbed into her own bed, having no trouble falling asleep.

CHAPTER 16

She woke with a warm lump nestled against the backs of her knees. Emilie lifted her head, twisting to see her unexpected bedmate. Soulful mahogany eyes returned her gaze, thick tail thumping against the covers. *Thwack, thwack, thwack.*

"So the dog bed was a ruse, was it? I guess we know where you sleep." She chuckled, pushing upright and reaching to stroke Holly's pretty head. "Don't let me disturb you."

Her bathrobe wasn't as warm as the bed, which was extra-cosy with the new canine heater. It was oh-so-tempting to crawl back to it after visiting the bathroom. But even though it was Christmas morning, there was a farm full of horses waiting to be fed. Horses didn't care about holidays. So she pulled on her layers of leggings and sweatpants, base layer and hoodie, braiding her hair. Holly rolled onto her belly, watching.

"I don't know what I'm going to do with you, but we'll start by letting you out. Let's go, Christmas dog."

Holly rose, and landed on the floor with a solid thud, following Emilie downstairs like a baby duck latching onto her new mother. Emilie was sure she was being so easy because she was a little insecure in her new environment, but it was so sweet. Oh, her heart was long gone to this dog. It had been like a sponge waiting to mop up all that sweet Labrador essence.

There would be time later for a long walk and play out in the snow, but for now, she only gave Holly a few minutes to relieve herself.

"Breakfast, maybe?" she said, rifling through the canvas bag of toys and supplies. The stainless steel bowls she found had little paw prints etched on them. This dog had special things. She'd been loved in her other life. That made Emilie happy, but sad, too. She must miss her person. "I'll try to make up for it, Holly dog."

In case she had any doubts Holly was a Labrador, the black dog hoovered up her kibble in a breath, then looked up as if she was expecting seconds.

"Sorry, I don't fall for that one. Just ask Twizzle," Emilie said. "Norma pointed out you could lose a couple of pounds. But, I'll make you a deal." She searched in the bag again and found a bag of green chews that were supposed to help keep dogs' teeth clean. "If you go in your house, you can have one of these."

The perfect dog padded to the living room and into her crate, turning around to pop her head out expectantly, tail thumping against the sides. Emilie handed her the treat, which Holly took with amazing daintiness.

"You really are too much." Emilie laughed and secured the door.

She made herself eat a Kashi bar, making sure Holly seemed settled in the crate before leaving for the barn. Claire and Chique greeted her as if she was late, which she was not. She put hay outside for them while they ate their breakfast. Both of them inhaled the feed almost as fast as the Labrador, so, leading them out in the dark, she put them in their paddock then moved on to the training barn.

There were no less than five cars outside. When she squeezed in through the doors, shutting them behind her, Jillian, Ava, Deanna, and Kyrie stood outside the break room with rope shanks in their hands. Who was the fifth? She grinned when he appeared from the feed room: Chip, an exercise rider from the track who had started their yearlings this year.

"Why are you all here?" She asked, though she couldn't stop smiling.

"We agreed we'd rather all come today than muck two days' worth tomorrow," Kyrie said.

"But what about you, Chip?"

He shrugged. "Dean told me what was up. I'm happy to lend a hand."

Emilie grinned. "They're fed already?"

"Yep." Kyrie nodded. "Except for Chique and Claire, because we figured you'd do them."

"And the big boys are out," Chip said.

"What about your families?" Emilie asked.

"It's just how it worked out this year," Kyrie said.

"I always used to go help muck out on Christmas Day at the boarding barn where I kept my horse," Ava said. "So I'm in."

"I needed an excuse to get out of the house for a few hours," Deanna said, and Jillian nodded.

"You sound like my sister." Emilie laughed, then turned to Chip.

"I'm an orphan," he said.

"You are not." Emilie laughed, swatting him lightly across the legs with the shank.

"Okay. I was going to be on my own, anyway. I'm not

seeing my daughter till tomorrow. Kid gets like three Christmases. C'mon. Grab a shank. Let's get these horses out."

It felt so good, even if it was just for a few minutes, not to be the one making the decisions. To have the others dictate this was how it was going to be and all she had to do was shut up and accept it. It was the best present anyone could have given her. Next to Holly, of course.

The coffee was ready by the time the horses were out, and Chip backed the tractor and spreader into the training barn. They only took a quick break before tackling the stalls, everyone in a happy, high-energy mode. She kind of wished they did things like this every day — work until the stalls were done — but she'd conceded the first and second coffee breaks contributed to staff morale, and keeping them happy was more important than her need to get things done promptly. Otherwise, she'd be doing it all herself. That was all the reminder she needed.

"That has to be some kind of world record," Jillian laughed as she swept up the last barn.

"Good to know we can do it that fast if we need to," Kyrie said.

"Feels wrong to bring them in this early, though," Emilie said. She was ready to tell them to all go home, and she'd do it on her own later so the horses could have a regular day out. The stalls would be less of a mess tomorrow that way.

"By the time we finish brunch, it won't be so bad," Kyrie said.

Emilie laughed. Kyrie had to be joking. "Brunch?"

Chip nodded, put away the last pitchfork, and steered her toward the door. "I'm famished."

All of them packed into Chip's beat-up old four-door Dakota.

"But, are there enough seatbelts in here for all of us?" Emilie asked, wedged between Ava and Jillian.

"We're not going far," Chip said. And he drove to the house.

The Corolla parked in front of it was very familiar. Emilie cast a sideways look at the others as they climbed the steps to the front door, all of them grinning foolishly. Secret-keepers, every one. Faye had taken over the kitchen, the counters loaded with food.

Emilie took it in with wonder. "How did you get into my house?"

"We've always had a key to your house, Em. You didn't know that?"

She shook her head silently. "What can I do?"

"You can sit yourself down with the others and get ready to eat."

Will passed out cappuccinos to everyone in cups from Triple Shot. "I can't believe you don't have an espresso machine, Em."

"Why would I when I'm at the café every day? Did you actually drive there to make these?"

"Yep. Faye and Dean don't have one either. Gonna have to do something about that." He winked at Faye.

Gus's arrival on the scene seemed belated, Faye and Dean's big Golden Retriever bouncing up to Emilie. "Where were you? I bet I can guess." Emilie laughed. "You were visiting with Holly."

"Who's Holly?" Ava asked.

"My new dog!" Emilie smiled so big her face hurt.

"Are you going to introduce us?" Dean asked. "C'mere Gus. I'm sure she doesn't need your nosey face in hers."

Not needing to be asked twice, Emilie skipped to the living

room. She let the Labrador into the backyard first before returning to the kitchen. Holly wasn't as outgoing as Gus, following Emilie with a modicum of caution, then greeting each human respectfully in turn. Gus sat next to Dean, barely contained, and it shocked Emilie he was showing any restraint at all.

Once she'd said hello to the people, Holly sashayed up to Dean, Gus whining pitifully. Holly sniffed him, tail wagging.

Emilie shrugged. "Let's see how it goes."

Holly warmed up to Gus in a heartbeat, falling for the Golden's charm like everyone else. In a few minutes, they were playing bitey face on the living room carpet.

Content the dogs were getting along, Emilie settled back onto the bench in the kitchen and turned to Will. "Are you moving into the farmhouse?"

"Faye's still deciding if that's okay. Dean's fine with it."

"What is your problem, Faye?" Emilie stared at her.

"I can't bear the thought of him giving up that amazing loft downtown. I'm attached to it. Besides, where will their band get together and play?"

"Uh, Will..." Emilie started, "you and Nate have been talking, haven't you?"

"Yep."

"About what?" Faye tilted her head suspiciously.

"Part of the reno on the house here. A music room." Emilie grinned.

"Are you renting an apartment to him, too?" Faye said. "I'm not sure I'm ready to live under the same roof as you." Her smile as she met Will's eyes gave away the lie.

"If he wants a job as farm manager, he gets a house with it," Emilie said.

"I'll take it, as long as I don't have to handle those stallions," Will responded

"Hmm," Emilie said. "Kind of a big part of the job, sorry. Guess you two better sort it out."

"Maybe I should take the job," Dean said. "If my sister is worried that the house isn't big enough for three."

"Don't tease me, Dean!" Emilie said. "I'll be plotting ways for you to be a remote trainer five months of the year."

Brunch was amazing. Emilie was so stuffed afterward she could have passed out on the couch. "Let's get the horses in so you all can go. I can't thank you enough, every last one of you."

"We'll head home after we're done cleaning up," Faye said, filling the dishwasher. "Will's mother is in town, so we're having her over. You're welcome to come, Emilie."

"Thanks, Faye." She squeezed her friend tight, hoping she conveyed the overflowing gratitude she felt. "I'm going to spend some time getting to know Holly. I'd feel terrible leaving her in the crate for the rest of the day after everything she's been through."

"Call me later, then. We've got things to talk about. I spoke with Sylvie, and she wants to help me out at the café."

"That's great news," Emilie said. "Honestly, Faye, it's not that I don't love it, but —"

"I know, Em. And you'll still keep your nose in things, I'm sure. Also, going by the budding romance between those two," Faye said, nodding at Gus and Holly, "we might want to plan a play date sometime soon. Maybe the usual drinks on Boxing Day?"

"Sounds perfect. I'll text you later about a time."

Ava, Jillian, Deanna, and Kyrie left once they brought in the weanlings. Only the stallions and Claire and Chique remained. Chip still insisted he had nowhere to be and said he'd help with them.

"About the manager job..." Chip began.

It would make her day if Chip said he'd take it. The ideal end to a hellish week. "You'd be perfect, Chip."

He laughed. "Naw. Sorry Em, but there's too much *farm is a four-letter word* in my blood for that. I'd let you down, and you've been let down enough. But a good friend of mine is thinking of relocating from Alberta. She's great. Has a ton of experience. A real solid horsewoman. I've told her about your situation, and she's excited by the prospect. Can I tell her to call you?"

"Please. And thank you. For that, and today."

When everyone was gone, this time, she didn't feel alone. She finally had time to make the call to Norma, who was ecstatic, immediately agreeing Holly should be hers. Then she took Holly outside and snapped on the longe line she'd brought from the training barn.

"Want to go for a walk, Holly? Let's go for a walk!" Holly bounced from her front paws. She knew that word, no question. "Let me give you a tour of the farm."

They romped around through the deep snow in the front yard first. Holly was sticking close, too excited by Emilie to care about anything else, and it made her heart want to burst. She flopped into the soft powder and made a snow angel, except Holly pounced on her, smothering her face with wet dog kisses so Emilie had to wrap her arms around the Lab and roll her out of the way to get up.

"Doesn't look much like an angel at all," she said, laughing.

They walked along the access road, past the track and the stallion barn and the vacant manager's cottage, then took the horse path through the woods. Holly's nose went to the ground, and more than once Emilie had to unsnag the line from low branches. They strolled between the empty paddocks on the other side of the forest, past the other barns, back to the house. Emilie didn't want it to end. She let herself daydream of easier days. Of Chip's friend being a fit for the farm and taking the job. Of having time to ride and train Holly to be a farm dog and go with her on hacks with Reba.

After such a huge meal earlier in the day, she didn't feel she was missing out by having soup and crackers and cheese for dinner. She called her parents afterward, then went to do night check, taking Holly with her. No drama tonight. Happy horses all.

With warmth emanating from the gas stove downstairs, she put on a movie and curled up with Holly on the couch. The black Lab had already so seamlessly assimilated herself into Emilie's life. It was as if she'd always been there. A match made in heaven. Meant to be. She kissed the top of Holly's head and hit play on the remote, but didn't get past the opening credits before her phone rang. It was Liv. Emilie had completely forgotten to call. FaceTime, no less. She was pretty sure the only time Liv had ever FaceTimed her was the year she'd stayed in Florida for Christmas.

Emilie grinned and accepted the call. Nate's face crammed next to Liv's in the frame.

"Merry Christmas!" she chimed. "Look what I've got!" She tilted the phone to capture Holly's head, resting comfortably on her knee.

"And here we've been worried because we hadn't heard from you," Nate said, grinning. "When did that happen?"

"Just last night. I was at Faye and Dean's and I got the call from a breeder I've been talking with. They were in a pinch and needed someone to foster, so I jumped."

"Foster," Liv said with a knowing smile. "Right."

"Yeah, she's already a foster fail. I feel like I'm twelve years old. She's just so perfect. Her name is Holly."

"So you're doing okay?" Liv asked.

"I won't lie — it's been a hard week. But today was brilliant. Everyone came and pitched in with the horses, and Faye and Will and Dean were over and made brunch for everyone, and Holly met Gus. And Chip has a lead on a manager!" She knew she was gushing like a tween, but she didn't care. "How are things there?"

"Good," Liv said. "Different, but good."

Then Nate must've taken the phone from her, because he changed the angle so she saw his parents — and Tim — in the background.

"Hi Emilie! Merry Christmas! I want to see pictures of that dog!" Nate's mother said. Even his father was smiling.

She was sure she heard Nate grumble in the background, "Come say hello." Then Tim's face came closer.

"Hi Emilie. Merry Christmas. What my mom said about the dog."

The view went back to just Nate and Liv, Nate shaking his head at his minimally communicative brother, but it was a baby step, in Emilie's mind. She'd take it.

"I guess we'll be seeing you in not too long," Nate said.

"Claire's good?" Liv asked, Emilie surprised she'd lasted that long.

"Yes, she's great."

"And no more excitement with Twizzle?"

"No, thank goodness."

"What are you doing tonight, then?"

"We'd just settled down to watch a movie when you called." Emilie squeezed Holly gently.

"Well, we'll leave you to it, then. Miss you," Liv said in parting.

"I miss both of you, too. Thanks for calling."

She felt a little strange; a little sad for a moment after disconnecting. The day had been so full, she'd forgotten how weird it was her family wasn't around. Her parents understood she couldn't leave the farm after Austin had quit, and she knew Nate and Liv needed to be in Calgary with his parents this winter. For a moment, she felt melancholy again. Then Holly nudged her nose under Emilie's hand and licked it.

"You're right. I have you. And we have a movie to watch."

She loved all the sappy holiday films Liv hated. She'd watch them all night, or at least until she fell asleep. Halfway through, she paused it to get snacks, Holly following her upstairs to the kitchen. Her phone chimed, and she remembered she'd meant to call Faye. It was too late now; she'd send a text instead.

But it wasn't Faye. It was a Facebook notification. A friend request, from Timothy Miller.

Huh.

That piqued her curiosity. She opened the app. Why not? Another baby step. She accepted it, closed the app, and sent Faye a message asking what time she wanted her there tomorrow.

She arranged herself on the couch again after hitting play — Holly under one arm, a bag of Cheetos in the other. Her phone chimed again. She ignored it. She wasn't going to be a slave to her notifications. She'd keep watching. Except her curiosity got to her again. She paused the movie, getting fake cheese dust all over the remote, and grabbed her phone from the end table.

A message now, from Tim. Well.

Great dog.

The man was clearly a brilliant conversationalist.

Thank you, she responded.

I think we got off on the wrong foot in Florida. Sorry.

If that's what you want to call it. She wasn't going to say it was okay. He was basically rude.

I meant it, he continued. *My brother with his stupid set up. I know that's what he's doing. So sorry for that too. I'm just...*

It was like he'd sent it by mistake, because it ended there. She wasn't going to let him ruin her perfect day. Time to go back to the movie with her new best friend.

I have to go, Tim. Merry Christmas, she typed.

I get it. I just wanted to say... I'm not like Nate. I'm not good with girls. And I have to put hockey first, anyway. But... maybe we could be friends? Like if I write... you'll write back?

It shouldn't have gotten to her. It felt like high school, and she was so beyond that. But it was Christmas, and everyone had been so nice to her today, and she had this amazing dog, and felt like everything was going to work out. So it was only fair to take his awkward little olive branch, wasn't it? It was cute. He wanted to write. Internet pen pals. There was no harm in going along with that.

Heavy sigh. (She wrote that, exactly.) *Okay. Yes. But I'm going now.*

Merry Christmas Emilie.

She realized she was smiling when she set the phone back down. What a silly little exchange. He really did act like he was fifteen. But she had a sister who wasn't the best at communicating with people, though Liv was getting better. It took practice, just like anything. So she had to give the guy a break. And writing messages back and forth, if it happened, seemed pretty safe.

She went back to the movie, feeling the comforting weight of the Lab against her. At the beginning of the week her favourite holiday had turned into a day she'd been dreading as the world collapsed around her, but it had turned out to be so completely wonderful — with just enough weird, after that exchange with Tim — to remind her it was reality, not a dream.

148

This wasn't how the romance novel of her life was supposed to end. But this wasn't the end at all, was it?

Holly licked her hand again, then peered up at her with those big, warm eyes. It wasn't so bad being alone on Christmas — because she wasn't alone at all.

THE END

THANK YOU!

Keep turning the pages to read chapter one of *All The Best Things*, the next book from the world of Triple Stripe, for the continuation of Emilie's story, now available.

Emilie's finally graduated, with a great job and a schedule that lets her enjoy horses on her terms. She spends her mornings riding ex-racehorses so she can find them new careers, her evenings working at the physiotherapy clinic and comes home to her sweet black Labrador Holly, who she adopted at Christmas. Her life is settled — until her brother-in-law invites Tim to the farm to recover from a hockey injury and turns her world upside-down.

Merry Little Things runs parallel to *This Good Thing (Good Things Come Book Four)*, which continues Liv and Nate's story. If you haven't read it, you can get it in e-book and print at your favourite retailer.

Reviews on your favourite retailer, as well as on BookBub are always appreciated. They feed authors, which lets us keep writing more books for you. It doesn't have to be long — pick some stars and write a few words!

For news on latest releases, free books, sample chapters and a peek into my life be sure to sign up for my newsletter at https://www.lindashantz.com/writes

I would be remiss if I didn't say a few words about ovarian cancer awareness. Symptoms are often vague and mistaken for other issues. If you're a woman experiencing any of these symptoms and they're new, persistent, or frequent, please consult with your doctor. Early detection is important!

- Bloating
- Abdominal pain or discomfort
- Fatigue
- Urinary symptoms
- Changes in bowel habits
- Difficulty eating
- Unexplained weight loss or weight gain
- Menstrual irregularities

Information source: https://ovariancanada.org/About-Ovarian-Cancer/Detection/Signs-Symptoms

ALL THE BEST THINGS
CHAPTER ONE

I f someone had chosen to write the novel of her life, this is not the storyline they would have gone with, but Emilie loved her life. It wasn't perfect, but what was?

She loved being the last to leave the physiotherapy clinic where she worked, shutting down her computer after updating her patient notes; turning off the lights, locking the clinic door behind her. She loved her trusty Honda Civic, hopping in it for the short drive home. She loved the eclectic playlist she sang along with for the short drive home, and she loved her brother-in-law for putting it together for her. He had the best taste. In music and in women, because he had, of course, married her sister.

She loved the farm she shared with them, where she got to indulge in her passion — retraining retired racehorses for new careers — and they got to indulge in theirs, breeding and training those Thoroughbreds for the races.

She loved her dog, the happy black Lab she'd adopted Christmas Eve, Holly, bouncing enthusiastically in welcome at the door when she entered her apartment, ready to go for their daily romp at dusk. As long as Emilie didn't mention food. If she did, Holly would dive back into her kennel, no matter how badly she had to go, waiting till Emilie served up a treat.

She loved this time of night. It wasn't her favourite — that would always be dawn — but there was something magical about the spectrum of orange deepening to indigo as it curved away from the horizon after the sun had dropped below it to the gentle music of the cicadas and frogs.

The novelist would no doubt have written in a love interest, but while her own attempts at real-life plotlines had come up short, a man with any sort of commitment attached to him had proved unnecessary for her to feel fulfilled. She had enough. The good job, the satisfying hobby, great family and friends, and Holly the Labrador. If Mr. Right came along tomorrow, she wouldn't chase him away, but she wasn't waiting for him. She was living her life, with or without him.

She wandered around the farm with Holly, some of the horses tucked into their stalls, others wispy shadows in the fields behind white stud rails. She didn't even mind the mosquitoes. Okay, she did. They were aggravating. Holly didn't seem to care, though.

The June days were warm enough most of the horses lived outside this time of year and came in for the hottest hours of the day. The exceptions were the layups from the racetrack and her project horses, all of which lived in the training barn and she switched on the lights to the tune of their hopeful nickers. Night check had been done by the farm manager two hours ago, but Emilie's nightly walkabout was extra assurance that all was well on the property.

She peeked in the stalls where the occupants' heads didn't immediately appear over the gate yokes, the attentiveness of those who did rewarded with a peppermint treat. The others dozed, her arrival not enough to rouse them.

This one was on stall rest, a post-operative case following knee surgery to remove chips. That one was starting back into carefully scheduled work as part of rehabilitation for tendonitis. Her project ponies waited expectantly. None of them would ever miss out on their late-night treat.

First was Excursion, an older gelding born and raised on the farm, recently retired after a solid career. He'd been the farm's hopeful one year for the Queen's Plate, Canada's most famous race — four years ago now, was it? Now he was ready for a new career.She had a riding lesson on him set up for Friday. She hadn't taken a lesson in years. Time in the saddle when she'd been in school had meant helping gallop the horses at the racetrack or teaching the newly off-track horses the very basic-basics, nothing more advanced. She was excited. And terrified. It was going to be great.

Next was Miss Talk About It, a five-year-old mare she'd taken on for New Chapter, the local Thoroughbred retirement group. Volunteering for New Chapter had been Emilie's pet project for a few years. Last fall when their parents had decided to move back to Montreal, her sister Liv had agreed that Emilie should make a stall or two available for overflow from New Chapter's home base farm. Miss Talk About It was the first. Someone was coming tomorrow to try her. If that was her person, another horse waited to fill the stall.

The dark face of one of the racetrack layups appeared, attracted by the crunch of peppermints. He craned his neck over the stall gate hopefully. Trop was a three-year-old colt who had yet to run a race and Liv had sent him home for a brief holiday when she'd decided to geld him. He was a brat, always ready with a quick nip and his inability to focus on training the way he should had earned him that appointment with the vet.

Emilie grinned as he dove for the peppermint, keeping her palm flat and her fingers safe. "Your cuteness is a problem." She swept his generous forelock to the side to take in the ever-present mischief in his big dark eyes.

She flipped off the bright fluorescents and left the barn, a yard light high on a hydro pole flooding the immediate area. Holly snuffled along the edges of the laneway as she walked out of its domain. The two mares in the big pasture to Emilie's right, near a small barn that housed the farm office, picked up their heads at the motion of woman and dog, and the smaller, darker one rumbled a greeting. Chiquenaude, the horse Emilie credited with bringing Liv and Nate together. That was as much of an accomplishment as the wins and earnings the mare had accumulated at the track. Now Chique was officially a broodmare, in foal with her first, due the end of January.

Passing the house she shared with Liv and Nate, Emilie headed to the back of the property along the lane next to the training track. It was dark here, nothing artificial to illuminate her path, but the lack of light pollution made it the perfect place to stop and throw her head back. She stared up at the expanse of the sky. It always made her feel like a child again, counting the brighter, steadier planets amid the endless tiny, flickering pinpricks of the stars. It might make a girl feel lonely and small. But it didn't. Instead, it felt like a hug; a reminder things were fine exactly how they were. She breathed in and threw her arms wide... then swatted at a mosquito. Holly ran back to her from whatever scent she'd been engrossed in and Emily propelled herself forward again, the Lab a prancing, companionable presence at her side.

How could she complain about her life? About this magnificent sky, this beautiful farm, those wonderful horses, her amazing family. They even, finally, had a great farm manager who everyone adored. She didn't need a man to be complete. For once, everything felt settled.

The stallion barn was quiet, but she walked through just to be sure. Just Lucky, who topped the sire ranks in Canada right now, napped in his deep bed of straw, all curled up with his nose resting on the golden cushion. So cute when he was sleeping, but he was a rascal when he was awake — just like his son, Trop. Next door, Starway, no slouch in the breeding shed himself, stood with hip hitched, one hind leg cocked, resting but aware. Both had hay and water, so she left them to it.

Kerrie's cottage was dark, the manager probably asleep. She'd have all the horses fed before the staff arrived at seven in the morning so she went to bed religiously at ten, except on those occasions she joined in on the fun of a bonfire or barbecue with the staff. Kerrie had initiated those events; just part of the above and beyond that made her such a perfect addition to the farm.

The main house was also dark when Emilie returned, save for a light in the kitchen. Nate and Liv would be fast asleep by now too, because they were up even earlier than Kerrie to head into the racetrack. Emilie passed through her apartment to the door that opened into the main part of the house because, even though the apartment had a kitchenette, Nate was a better cook than she was, and when their schedules didn't allow her to join him and Liv for dinner, Nate usually left her something in the fridge. She was always hungry after she and Holly walked, the short-term benefit of the snack-size yogurt she'd scarfed down at work a few hours ago long since gone.

Holly bounded ahead of her, disappearing around the corner to the indistinct murmur of a voice. Clearly the kitchen wasn't empty.

"Hey, Nate. What are you still doing up?"

Her brother-in-law sat at the breakfast nook, flipping absently through something on his phone with one hand while he scratched Holly behind the ears with the other. He lifted his head, smiling, his blue eyes tired, and dropped his phone on the table to run fingers through his blond hair as he yawned.

"On the phone to Calgary," he said.

As soon as Emilie dipped into Holly's food container, the Lab abandoned him, diving into her stainless steel bowl before Emilie even set it on the stone tile of the kitchen floor.

"Everything all right?" Emile asked as she opened the fridge and spotted the leftover salad and salmon waiting for her. She set it on the counter and opened one of the drawers for cutlery. Should she heat up the salmon, or just dive right in?

"Oh yeah," he assured her. "Time difference is all. I was talking to Tim."

She felt his eyes on her when he tacked on that last bit, waiting for a reaction. She wasn't going to give him one.

When Nate had started working on the farm almost six years ago now — where had the time gone? — Emilie's playful crush had turned into an easy friendship. As soon as everyone learned he had a younger brother, they'd all decided she and Tim were meant to be. She'd let herself believe it, for a while. Why not? If he was as good-looking and kind as Nate, she was in.

Except he wasn't. Sure, he was seriously attractive — more so, even, than Nate. He had a body any girl would swoon over, thanks to being a professional hockey player. But the rest of it? The whole nice guy thing? Nope. All the looks in the world didn't make up for what he lacked.

Even after he'd given her the cold shoulder at Liv and Nate's wedding, she'd thought there might be a chance when, for some reason, he'd friended her on Facebook on Christmas Day. And for some reason, Emilie had accepted. She was convinced it was because of Holly, who she'd introduced to Nate and Liv while FaceTiming them when they were in Calgary for the holiday. Tim had appeared on-screen reluctantly to say a no-doubt coerced hello, but the smiling Labrador had brought out something resembling warmth. They'd started a cute back-and-forth correspondence through Messenger. It had been fun, for a few months.

Then he'd ghosted her.

So he'd been sent back to the minors after a stint playing for the Flames — Calgary's NHL hockey team. But nothing? Really? Not a peep.

So, that was done. She was all for second chances, but she'd given him that. A third one would just make her look like an idiot. No, thank you.

She didn't hate him. She didn't feel enough of anything for him to invest in that kind of grudge. The best thing about all of it was that he was thousands of miles away. These days, he barely even entered her thoughts.

"And how is Tim?" she asked, crossing her arms and leaning back against the counter.

Nate put his usual ready smile on hold. "The injury's got him down. I know the season's over, but he's pretty dedicated. He's not dealing so great with not being able to train."

She'd felt bad, really she had, when Tim had hurt his knee in a game with the farm team, necessitating surgery to repair the torn ACL. It had to suck, working that hard and hoping to get another chance at the big time, only for that to happen. Knees were tricky. She saw similar cases all the time at the clinic. Healing right took a lot of patience.

"Like brother, like brother?" she quipped.

Nate's lips twisted in a wry grin. "Smartass."

Last summer Nate, a jockey, had been the injured one, the back trauma he'd suffered in a spill at the historic Saratoga Racetrack earning him his own surgery and subsequent time off and rehab. Somehow he'd worked through it and now, here he was, happily married to her sister and back riding at the top of his game, recently adding the richest race on the planet, the Dubai World Cup, to his list of career achievements. At least he'd become an adult.

Which included not teasing Emilie about Tim anymore, something she was grateful for. He had to know they'd stopped talking, didn't he? Or maybe he was just too wrapped up in his own life as a newlywed and leading rider to concern himself with hers.

"You want anything?" She took the water jug from the fridge and poured herself a glass, then, after setting the glass and bowl on the table, sat across from him.

"Nah. I need to get to bed." He slid to the end of the bench behind the kitchen nook and stood, phone in his hand, then paused in the doorway. "I invited him to come out for a bit. The change of scenery will do him good."

"You *what?*"

The reaction she'd so effortlessly avoided after the initial mention of Tim's name charged back in like a dancing bear.

"I figure he can stay in my old apartment, seeing as it's empty at the moment." Nate's tone stayed casual, but his eyes continued to gauge her carefully.

Really, what could she say? *Why didn't you ask me first? This is my home too. No, he can't come. Or if he does, tell him to bring a bodyguard, because I can't promise I won't try to kill him.* Jerk. Tim, and his brother too.

"See you tomorrow Em."

As soon as Nate slipped away, Emilie dumped the rest of

her water down the drain and found a bottle of wine, from which she poured herself a generous portion.

So, she was wrong about Tim. She did hate him.

THANKS FOR READING! *You can order the e-book or paperback from your favourite store now or ask for it at your library!*

Nanaimo Bars Recipe

Like the butter tarts featured in **All The Little Things,** Nanaimo bars are a distinctly Canadian treat. This recipe, which is the one I grew up with, is not as sweet as some versions, but they're delicious just the same! If you try them, let me know what you think.

Preheat oven to 350°F.

BASE:

Melt:

- 1/2 cup butter
- 1/4 cup white sugar
- 3 tablespoons cocoa

Stir and add:

- 1 beaten egg

- 1 teaspoon vanilla

Add:

- 2 cups vanilla wafer crumbs
- 1/2 c walnuts
- 1 cup coconut

Press above into lightly greased 8 x 8 pan and bake for 10 minutes. Let cool in pan.

FILLING:

Mix:

- 1/4 cup butter
- 2 cups icing sugar
- 1 tablespoon custard powder
- 1 tablespoons hot water

Spread on first layer and refrigerate for 1 hour.

TOPPING:

Melt:

- 2 squares (2 ounces) unsweetened chocolate (semi-sweet can be substituted for a slightly sweeter version)
- 1 tablespoon butter

Pour and spread over filling. Slice once topping is set, and store in refrigerator.

Acknowledgments

Special thanks go to my dear friend Juliet Harrison, who re-shared the details of her journey from ovarian cancer diagnosis through treatment and recovery. Any errors are my own. I'm especially grateful that eight years later, you're beating the odds.

As always, I'm indebted to my beta readers, Allison Litfin, Bev Harvey, Nathalie Drolet, June Monteleone, and Dr. Kristen Frederick DVM.

And I'm always grateful to Michelle Lopez, author and business accountability partner, who helps keeping me on task and is always supportive.

About the Author

 I began working at the racetrack before I finished high school, and after graduating the following January, took a hotwalking job at Payson Park in Florida. Once back at Woodbine, I started grooming and galloping. While the backstretch is exciting, I found I was more at home on the farm — prepping and breaking yearlings, nightwatching and foaling mares. Eventually I started my own small layup/broodmare facility, and in the last few years I've transitioned into retraining and rehoming. Somewhere along the way I did go back to school and get a degree. I should probably dust it off and frame it one day!

I live on a small farm in Ontario, Canada, with my adopted off-track Thoroughbreds and a young Border Collie, and I'm probably better known for painting horses than writing about them — if you like my covers, check out my artwork at www.lindashantz.com

Made in the USA
Monee, IL
02 June 2024

59252756R00104